Pain in the Church

By

Rev. John D. Housewright

Order this book online at www.trafford.com
or email orders@trafford.com

Most Trafford titles are also available at major online book retailers.

Printed in Victoria, BC, Canada.

ISBN: 978-1-4269-2065-3

*Our mission is to efficiently provide the world's finest, most
comprehensive book publishing service, enabling every author to
experience success. To find out how to publish your book, your way, and
have it available worldwide, visit us online at www.trafford.com*

Trafford rev. 10/28/2009

 www.trafford.com

North America & international
toll-free: 1 888 232 4444 (USA & Canada)
phone: 250 383 6864 ♦ fax: 812 355 4082

Introduction

This book has been written with great pains not to offend anyone or to hinder any work of God through any denomination. Only one mother church has been mentioned due to the impact that it had on my life when I entered the Pentecostal movement. My hopes and prayers have been continually to reveal to all that the pain in the church can and should be eliminated. Church is the people within any congregation that we can not do without, but the pain can be stopped if we just care for others the way Jesus does. I have no doubt what-so-ever that God wanted this book wrote to minister to the people that have been hurt in like manner or many of the same ways that have been revealed. Complete perfection in the church may be very hard to find but there should be peace, hope, and happiness.

In any church you enter into you have broken the strand of perfection even if the ones already there insist they have arrived. Too often we see only the faults of our brothers and sisters and find that we can not work with them. By this type of look at our fellow Christians we miss much needed help that God has provided to each of us. I believe that it is a shame to overlook such blessings. It is time to do our part to help stop the pain in the church.

Chapter One

How God Led Me Here

In 1985, after a shipwrecked life, two failed marriages and the loss of my mother, it was time to Examine my soul. Eighteen months in Vietnam left me with a lot of pain and stress that plagued me constantly. There had to be some kind of change or it was time to check into a mental institute. Since I did not like that idea at all, thought that I would do as my EX mother-in-law suggested. She would say that there was a pew down at the church that had my name on it. So I went to see! Sure enough that was for me! Wish that I could say that ended all my problems but that would be a lie. It did give me someone to spend the rest of my life in fellowship with, Jesus.

Working midnights at a motel gave me plenty of time to study the Word of God. Our precious Lord told me what I would learn in the dark, I would use in the light. So I poured myself into the Bible every night, studied according to subjects with some reading and a lot of prayer. It was not a duty but it was fun as God just opened up the scripture like I had never seen it before. There was no confusion but not many people wanted to help me without it costing something. Normally it was a price I would not pay. Yet there was a friend or two that made a difference. These very special children of God are still there for me today some twenty two years later.

Having quite a bit of time to study, I spent hours watching and seeking scripture with TBN. This caused me to hunger for the truth and the movement of the Spirit. However in the main line Denominational churches this Holy Ghost stuff was a little too much. In a very short time I began teaching God's Word in Sunday school. Being so young in the Lord most could not understand what God was doing with me. Yet quickly after a woman that was nearly blind received a healing to 20/20 vision, they asked me to leave and go to Pentecost. The statement was, "If we wanted to be Pentecostal we would go to that church." So, I left and went to the church across the tracks with the kind of mixed feelings most get when hurt.

The pastor realized that God wanted to use me and put me to work right away. I preached the next Sunday morning and took over as Sunday School Superintendent. He also sent me into the Children's Church, and things really started to happen. Bless their hearts they had not been taught that God does not do that anymore, so miracles began to happen. We went from six children to forty-six within the two years. From the beginning we started to have trouble with people trying to prove that

God was not doing the things that was spoken. There was a constant bombardment of criticism. I really could not see why the devil was in such a tizzy. I personally was not doing that much. Jesus was doing a great deal and He was working with signs and wonders, guess that was enough. Those two years there was eighty or so saved, baptized and filled with the Holy Ghost. That was a great ministry for our area. Yet the deacons finally shut down the ministry by removing the Pastor. Right away God said that my ministry was over there, so I moved on with a great deal of pain.

Even though I left the church across the tracks, there were some hard lessons. Never put your faith in man. Though we should be able to trust most all people, there must be an awareness of all that is going on around us. When God begins to move the jealousy is intended to provoke people to good works. Yet so often what happens is trying to make ourselves look better by making those God is using look bad. This is to the failure of teaching the Word with true conviction and sincere knowledge of it. Can we get the idea that when we hurt someone else we hurt the Sweet Holy Spirit that lives within us? It is time we learned this lesson without the pain it can cause.

Here is one of the events that happened to me that someone may be able to explain. There was this couple in the church that had been praying for the Baptism in The Holy Ghost for several years. Maybe it was the simplicity of teaching that made this event so hard to come by or just the lack of knowledge. Either way it really did not matter to me. All I could see was that they have done all they should do to receive. After watching this man struggle so hard at the same alter for a solid week I felt that maybe I could help. So I asked if I could come over and talk with them for a little while. We went right after church on a Thursday night. There was about one hour of talk about how to receive and one thirty second prayer. This dear saint went out praying in tongues. Now after this day, this couple would not talk to me at all. Each time the preacher asked me to preach they would get up, right in front of the whole church and walk out. They refused to talk to me or anyone else. Why may be something that I take to my grave, never understanding?

In my twenty years of service to our Lord, I have found many things hard to explain and much that can not be. When these things get out of control, we must turn to the one that can do something with us, Jesus. Here is a twenty year old lesson, when something is wrong; you may be able to change it; you may not be able to change it; and or you can always pray and give it to Jesus. When we do we no longer hinder God's work and usually that is when the movement of God continues to reach souls with a new enthusiasm.

After we left this church, there were about twelve of us that wanted to gather together. Our pastor went back to his home church in the area, so we began meeting in a home for services. In our second meeting the Lord said he wanted us to begin a church of our own. With his promise that he would prosper us, we started meeting on the times of regular church services. In that meeting there was a man that had a family of three and I that was called of God to Preach. I tried everything to talk him into being the Pastor but he would not. They told me to start it and see where God leads us. So as a single man we began the church. From Wednesday night to Sunday morning the Lord had given us a name, a charter, and most of the bylaws. Since God brought all this through me, it was easy to see why they called me to pastor. Fearfully I began the work and had a blast in doing the job. This was not hard but it was fun all the time. We received our tax exemption a lot sooner than normal and everything seemed to fall into place. Moving to a store front building was the best solution for our group to serve our Lord Jesus. At least that was what we thought.

It did not take very long to receive a piano, cassette player, and an eight channel mixer. Speakers and two cheap mikes, we were in business. We had been praying and fasting for the will of God, so it did not surprise us when the Lord took off. Souls were saved, people received the Baptism in the Holy Ghost and others received their deliverance. What a great time we had! Our classrooms divided up and soon we had three classes for Sunday school. With three services per weak, we were just not happy enough. There is really something to say for being hungry for more of the Lord. A Monday night bible study did seem to fill the bill. It was not long until we were running around forty people. Forty six was the highest number we had. When we reached that point something always happened and people would leave. We did not get below twenty for eight years. But it was hard fought!

In this building we found some real challenges. Prayer was the call to business on a daily bases. At first people were real reluctant to stay in a store front church. Most could not understand why we wanted to stay here. It seemed that it did not matter how we explained it not many would stay with us. Families would come in for a couple of weeks and then leave. I used to say that they got what they needed and moved on. Most people when to other churches. That usually does not bother a pastor much, as long as they are still going to church somewhere. Going to see them was usually a pleasure, and seldom was there a problem to address.

It was years on down the line that I found out that the people were not feeling at home because it was a family run church. What a shame, because we were not a family, we just worked very close together.

There were many causes for a loss of people, yet very little can we blame on anyone but ourselves. I believe that discernment was the greatest need and quite often it is the need in the churches I have visited. We do not like the idea that we did not know what is going on. So I have seen every excuse under the sun to explain the losses. Only too often do we hear that someone hurt our people? Some of it was accidental, some unintentional, but most of it was on purpose. There has to be one that lashes out to cause harm even when there is no cause what-so-ever. This one can range from the Pastor on down to the least in the church. What is really bad is that all of it can normally be avoided. Is it about time that we as a church change this into tranquility, unity and love like Jesus?

Here is one of the millions of example, we had a great couple in the church and they were very faithful. In their search for a closer walk with Jesus they started to pay allot of attention to each other's independence. In asking for the truth you would expect them to fine just that, right? Yet in her trying to find her freedom in The Spirit, she started seeing that her husband was not always right. She started questioning some of his answers and references to his behavior toward her. Maybe you have guessed it, someone jumps in there and suggest the pastor must be putting these ideas in her head. Do you realize that he left the church and nearly ended up in divorce? Because someone wanted to steel their liberty and stop such a great relationship that they had. Thank God they are still together, madly in love with each other, and do not take the other for granite any more. But there was that effort to destroy.

One of the many battles we do not want to face is the experience of a false prophet coming in to steal our liberty in Christ. Too often we tend to turn a deaf ear to what people say and do not take it serious enough. There were several people coming to me because of notes they were receiving during the services. This was very strange being a new church. It was assumed that we would not have a clue as to how to handle this problem. So according to the bible, I first went to them to see what the reason was behind the notes. This was of no effect, so I took my trustee with me. This also was no good and the notes kept coming behind my back. One morning it just seemed like this was all that The Holy Ghost was going to put up with. He prompted me to ask for all the notes that had been handed out. There were about forty some people there and about thirty notes to different adults. I started by declaring that there was no intent to harm anyone. Than I took each note and read them out loud. After I read them I asked each person if the note had any barring on their life. Needless to say none of the notes seemed to have any value. We then confronted the false prophet. This person had caused no little concern in the church, yet with this action, they left the place and have not been back. I would to God that they would have gotten right the invitation was given.

Other pain presented to the church, was that of false tongues and interpretations. You know that the gifts are for the unbelievers so it is very important to pay close attention to every word spoken in the church. This started out right and seemed like nothing was wrong with the statements at all. Every word given was to up-lift the Lord Jesus. After about two weeks the tongues started to get out of order and I called them down. Thinking this could have been their zeal for the Lord I let them continue as long as it was in order. The Holy Spirit never interrupts Himself, when that happens we should start to pray and ask why. Well I found out the next service! The tongues seemed way out, very different, and had a funny sound to them. Right off I tried the spirits to see where they were of God. Then we heard the answer as the interpretation declared that Jesus was in the room and He had sinned. If He could sin there would be no salvation! Calling the person down "In the Name of Jesus" Pleading the Blood of Jesus over the church and all at home I called out the "prophet's word" as false declared the truth and proclaiming how the tongues could not possibly be of God. That teaching became a two hour service and the false prophet has never come back. Can you imagine the amount of pain that caused the new believers and the time it took me to straighten out this mess?

This was extremely painful to so many of the younger Christians in the church! No one truly believed her yet they could not understand what caused such a thing to be allowed by God. When all you can do is hold on to the foundation of your faith, these kinds of things have a tendency to rattle your understanding. If we could just believe that our faith in the elders is steadfast and they will deal with this, then we can get past such a thing. This was my main theme of teaching on the matter. Yes, we explained every detail of tongues and interpretation, the gifts of The Holy Spirit, and the will of man to be heard, though the main need was not to trust something that was not in tune with the Bible. Anything false has nothing to do with God. Our salvation depends upon the perfect sacrifice of Jesus in the Blood Atonement and that a gift is to all who except and believe in Him. Sometimes I have found that we put too big an emphasis on a problem and not go back to the foundation to reestablish the basics.

When people want to do the right thing all the time, every time and not want to be the center of attention, we can have church without many of the fears of false tongues, or prophets. One of the largest desires to put under the Blood of Jesus is the recognition syndrome. In a church of forty you do not usually have five preachers sent to the same church. When this happens there is normally division. Since we all know that God is not the author of confusion also know that all these people can not be right. This is where politics often over rule God's intentions for that church. We often see with the eyes when God is looking at the heart and purpose. My experience with politics has left me hurting more times than not. Either for my losses or for someone else that got hurt in the process. There is a great need for holy people to fast and pray so as the will of God can accomplish the task. Only than can there be true peace in the House of God and service becomes what it should be, fun.

In a small church people see people for who they are not what they want to be. This often leaves people open for every kind of gossip and heartache. One particular way this comes is when people are a little strange and do not quite fit in to the swing of the church. With all our efforts to keep clicks from forming it still happens. When people can not quite stack up to their comparisons the pain flows even when it is unintentional, it still hurts. Example, be a woman six feet three inches tall. Then understand the weight discrimination of about three hundred and forty something. Add a little immaturity, and one that struggles with the scriptures and you see the potential of serious hurt in the church. At first everyone tries to pitch-in and make a difference in their life.

But that soon fades away to just good intentions. Also when there is demon possession and a continual battle it does not take long at all to find those truly dedicated to the Lord. Anytime this dear soul wants to be free from anything hindering them there would be complete deliverance available through the Blood of Jesus. When they need the attention of the spirits they think they controlled they walk away from the church in pain. In the defense of the church, they did try very hard for a while and the scriptural teaching was right. There is no way that this person could say they left without knowing the truth about deliverance. Jesus was able to meet every need they just did not want deliverance that bad. They rejected God, our prayers and the desire is that they will come to him before it is too late.

Too often people see what they want to, instead of what God intends for any church. As long as there is no conflict we feel that we are doing right somewhere I read that Jesus did not come to bring peace but a sword. Truly I believe that the meaning here is that when God has set certain things in order any which oppose such will find themselves fighting against Him. Then we have deep divisions. The statements I have heard the most is; anyone can hear from God, you may be wrong, or you may of missed God, does God speak to us too, we have heard what is right because we have the majority, and again, this can not be of God no one has that kind of faith. Here is the reason that Jesus said that He was the head of the church and his angels will hear his voice. This is also implying that they will obey the word of the Lord as well. There are few things in the church that hurts any more than to know the will of God and not be able to implement such. This breaks your heart and many times causes you to loose your confident in others.

In the older Pentecostal or main line Denominational we find that it was understood that The Man of God would hear from Him and lead in the right direction. Over the last twenty years I have seen this respect fall away fast. I dare to say it has been because of many a minister and also the lack of respect given. Even as late as five years ago you never heard the pastor's first name without; Pastor, Brother, or Rev... This failure has also been to the loss of many of the gifts in the church. When I was paying the price with fasting, prayers and bible study, there was never a lack of the gifts or respect. When I slacked off both were lost. Did I change that much? Did I deserve such? Can you see where I am going? For minister and saint alike there is a price to pay for the blessings of God to fall on any church. As we pay this price we will see true revival again and not just go through the motions. We also see too little prayer in everybody. If you really need for things to happen than ask God and make sure you do not quench the Holy Spirit so he can work things out? I truly believe that if we would spend more time directing people back to the right path instead of condemning them for their failures, than it would be possible to see a whole lot more of God's favor. You see, it is the Anointing that breaks the yoke of bondage and this comes through Holy Vessels directed by The Lord.

Another real pain in the church has become the continual bombardment of words spoken against the Anointed of God. I am quite aware that this comes from the devil yet it is the church members that carry the tails. When it is so easy to destroy one's reputation, why do so many "good people" spend all their time on such adventures? Lies spread are one of the most damaging.

Mainly because it is easier to believe a lie, than go to church to change your life. People use every excuse under the sun to keep from giving their lives over to The Lord. When they can look into the church and see how we can talk about each other than they can say that they are better than that so why bother with church. What really stinks is that the only way people can look good is to make others look bad. We have got that backward. We should live right so as to look good before all mankind, either publicly or in secret. So why lie on others? It is not going to get you into heaven and seldom will it get you the attention you want for more than about a minute. When can we see that if we do this to others, the ones we spread this to, will also talk about us. Come on church, let us admit it and quit it!

At one time there was a large push for everyone to receive the Slaying power of The Holy Ghost. This out cry was directed by The Lord and ministers everywhere were fasting and praying for God to use them. Fasting and prayer was the main key, not only for this gift to work in your life but for all that God has in store for you. Somehow this has been forgotten or it has become too hard for us to do. I am not sure of which is the most dominant yet it is sad that the younger generation can not see the great miracles of twenty years ago. The Slaying Power is a gift toward a means not the means. The intention is to get each person to the point that they can receive from God. When this gift is working in the church, most all receive easily. We see, so we believe! It is better to believe without seeing but the end results are a sign that the unbelievers will know that God is in the house to save and heal.

From the very beginning of our ministry the gifts have flown freely and continually anticipated. There has been a great deal of blessing that The Lord has brought our way by Him using us. Do not ever think that just because we have to suffer at the hands of others that there are not tremendous blessings that go along with every obedient act. Too often the pain that others create seems to over ride the emotions. This is when, I think, we forget who is in charge of the results of our ministry. As we reach maturity in the Word, we also should be able to see these attacks in a better light. When we do this we can often win over our emotions through our testimony and the sacrifice of Jesus' Blood to help us get or keep on the right track. Getting off track of God's will is worst than the pain created. Many want the gifts to flow but do not want to change their life style which often causes the pain to stop you from operating in freedom. Why this happens to hinder a child of God, well, maybe we have touched on it, should it happen, never!

The amazement of the gifts is something that gets the attention of the unbelievers as quickly as anything else I know. So many of the good people are trying to prove the gifts are not working in the church. When one experiences this power with God, it will never be denied again. One young man came into the church just to watch and see if it was for real. Could Jesus really make Himself known? This was the statement asked after the experience of the slaying power of The Holy Spirit. He came forward and stiffened up like a board, almost daring God to "knock him down". He did not expect all the conviction that led him into the sinner's prayer and except Jesus as a personal savior. Than the Lord "knocked him down" in the Spirit, with a conversation that he would not repeat. It was so personal that he considered it sacred and I am willing to wager that he has never forgotten it. He moved to California and still when I think of him, I can't help but having a good feeling of how personal Jesus could be.

The greatest miracle is and will always be salvation. When the angles in heaven begin to rejoice over one sinner, then all the earth and church should be rejoicing with this one. There is no other blessing as great as leading a person to Jesus. Then everyone can know just how real God can be with them. My greatest desire is to see a changed life because Jesus has taken up residence in their heart. On the other hand, the pain created by uncaring or insensitive people can devastate most anyone. When one lays out all the rules and regulations before there is even a relationship or before these rules can be brought into perspective by the Holy Spirit, it is just plain wrong. We must become more sensitive to others past history and understanding of the scripture before we lay all this on them. Most people that I have counseled that have been hurt by the church, will site this type of behavior. This runs people off. Let us catch the fish and then let God clean them up! Maybe we can avoid having so many people wait so much later in life before they deal with their soul.

Another great pain comes from an evil spirit called confusion. We seem to crowd around one to help them pray through. Too often one is saying hold on another is saying let go and others are just praying in an unknown tongue. The pour child trying to receive Jesus becomes so confused that they just give up. One tells them they are saved another tells them they did not get through because they did not get The Holy Ghost, one tells them keep on trying, another says is there sin in your life, and yet another tells them that it may take awhile before they learn what they are doing. I am just trying to express this and I feel confused! What a shame. Yes we need alter workers but we need them to be sensitive to The Holy Ghost and know what is keeping one receiving from God. I can not stress this enough, good intending people can work against the Lord by not hearing Jesus. Pray with them, uphold them, protect them from intrusion but let God lead you so you will know what this individual needs the most. None of us are alike, even though we may be similar and we all receive from God differently. Learn what to do by listening to the only one that can read their heart, His name is Jesus.

In the church I pastured there was this great movement of the Spirit for about eight years. There was not a single service that the Anointing of The Spirit was not there. And that is only bragging on Jesus! For no one individual can say that they deserve the blessing of The Lord always present. Truly it is to His Praise. The services were always anointed and the presence of The Lord made people stand up and take notice. This was something to this day, twenty years later that I am eternally grateful to The Lord. How any group of people could get tired of such a ministry is beyond me yet that is what I feel happened. When everything under the sun can cause conflict, then people are looking for a way out. None of us are perfect so if we will look hard enough we will find fault in all people. Even enough to call it quits in the church that God has called us to. When God moves with great intentions of saving the lost, there is always conflict and the attempt to stop the movement of God. Too often it is the Christians that stop God from moving.

Chapter Two

The Gifts of God Always Bring a Fight

I can remember in the little store front that the power of God was so strong that I would even leave the church for work at five minutes before eleven and the rest of the people would not leave until one or two A.M. Many a night we would go on for hours and never get tired of God's presence. At that time there were a lot of needs being met, not just feeling good. We were always amazed at the different ways God would supply the needs. Fasting and prayer seemed to go on continually. No one ever got sick by fasting because we did it according to the scripture. Great is the reward of the faithful was a beautiful way to live our lives. Why does it have to change? Why do we every have to quit enjoying the movement of God? When does it come to the point that we are not willing to pay the price for souls? What is wrong with us? We can not even blame it on sin. We just have to look at the intentions of our hearts and find that we just simply quit! How else could we explain believing the lies and giving up on building a church?

Just prior to leaving the store front, there was a rumor started in the church. It spread throughout the community like wild fire. It got back to me through some very close friends and other ministers in the area. During one service there were about forty six people there. Twenty some came forward in the alter call and some twelve or so were slain in the Spirit. The gift of prophesy was working continually and many were hanging on every word, as well as watching everything that was going on. That was where the accusation came in. Now what was really sick was that the one told this was constantly causing trouble in every church they went to and people still believed the lie. It is so sad that we become a child of the devil when we cause such pain. Yet this was the beginning of the church falling apart and getting to lazy to fight. The building we were meeting in was sold out from under us and we had to find another place to worship. Can you see what this little lie opened us up to? Yes, we left the church on a Sunday night and opened in a little church Wednesday night the same week, but the damage had begun.

How can a person continue in a church with a very heavy anointing on it and cause such pain? It is beyond me to try to out quests God in the purpose of such, but still I wonder. All over the USA and I am sure all over the world there are people assigned by Satan to destroy the works of God, especially those with such powerful anointing that will minister to hearts. Yet they stay on continually causing doubt, confusion and the fear of false or fake ministers. When can the body of Christ stand on their own feet and recognize such trouble and defend the innocent? We as ministers can misinterpret our Lord and we can fail to follow Him truly but normally when that happens the anointing also backs off. Where are the watchmen on the towers that should be there to aid them instead of judging and destroying the ministers? Where are the ones you can depend on for spiritual help without it being spread all over the community? Where are those that will not point a finger but will offer a shoulder and a heart to lean on during a battle? Are we, as a joint body, so afraid of association that we can not any longer help a minister in trouble? May I ask what happened to the ministry of reconciliation? When we fail to help are we failing the scriptures? What is even worst then this is when the minister is not doing anything wrong and the judgment still stands.

After this took place I found most all of our people in the church came to me with the same or similar results. Over and over I tried to resign and could not because of Jesus. You see, Jesus told me that an innocent man should never give in to Satan and allow him to shut down God's work. We would average from twenty to forty people each service. Now where you are at that may not seem like much. However across the world that is about the average size of a small church. Still the anointing was there and miracles were taking place every service.

Again I emphasize that the power of God was always there. Through the following years there were battles that seemed impossible to overcome yet God came through every time. Praise his holy name! The greatest sign that our Lord gave us was the incredible Peace. No matter what happened the peace of God would come over me and we were able to minister to anything that came up. Even those that people said hated me would sit back in amazement as The Lord used me to minister to their own family.

One of the great gifts the Lord bestowed on me was the ability to hear the Lord's voice inside others. This happened only at times that they needed to now that God was working in their heart. When I understood something that only this person and God knew, people would be amazed and turned to the Lord every time. Continually I would let everyone know that I do not have such ability. Only God could read the heart that has never been shared out loud. Normally it was in private, with one or two present that the individual trusted. Also the contents were as sacred as my own personal vows to God. Unless that person shared them with someone else, no one ever hear a word about it from me. These that Jesus ministered to, sat up and took notice. They were usually blessed beyond measure and walked away praising The Lord Jesus. Many say these gifts do not exist, yet they see the word of knowledge and the word of wisdom and deny these also. We really need to take the Bible for what it says and not what we want it to say. Do you agree?

A very personal event that took place in the church during an alter service when I did not preach the message. The service had been very anointed and yet very subdued. Music was always good and you could really feel the Holy Spirit. In the alter service all was pretty quiet. There was a lady across the isle form me that was praying silently. Her face was buried into the back of the pew as mine was across the isle. You could hear others praying and there were about one hundred and twenty people there for this service. I heard in my heart that this lady was speaking to the Lord and looked up to see if she had said it out loud. That is how clear it was to me! Not even her lips were moving and I could see her clearly. Thinking this to be so personal, I just went back to praying alone, and did nothing. Again the Lord brought these words back to me in a very powerful way. I'm not sure that I can explain this but I know the voice of The Lord. When the words came to me the third time I knew that I had to do what was expected of me. The word that came to me was this dear lady said in her heart that if God would tell Bro. John to come and lay his hand on her back she knew that God would heal her and she would not ever have the back trouble again. Well, I went across the isle, laid my hand on her back, she said the exact spot of the bulging disk and leaned over to her and spoke what God had given me. Simply did you ask God to have me laid my hand on your back and you would know that He would heal you and you would never have trouble with your back again? Well, this dear Saint of God came from sitting on her legs to a jump and shout in seconds. She leaped, shouted twisted, touched her toes and ran all over the church. Of course you know the rest of the church exploded in worship. We had nearly a four hour service and enjoyed it very much. Give Jesus all the praise for such a gift and love of His children.

Throughout the gospels there was the quote of Jesus knowing their hearts or He knew that they were setting a trap for them to catch him in a statement against the Law of Moses. Though they never did they marveled over His doctrine. To me that meant that He blew their mind. Today Jesus is still blowing peoples' minds. We make our statements of how exactly God has to move and He constantly does things differently yet better. When can we realize that He can see the future and knows what it will take to accomplish the task the most efficient way? When are we going to say your will not mine and mean it? Why not just believe and go on with Jesus? Is it so important that we put forth our great knowledge and stand out so? Now do not get angry with me but the Lord put it this way with me, "When will people glorify me for what I do for them?" Can you see the tears that Jesus sheds over how people open up their selves for an attack from Satan? You see when we glorify ourselves we open up the door for Satan because that is one of the "I will's" that he did to get kicked out of heaven. It would not be right for God to punish him and not us. Think about what you do before you cause such pain for yourself or others. Give all the praise and glory to Jesus in all things!

On the counter part of such a great miracle by Jesus there were those in the church that wanted to evaluate all of us. How could such a thing happen? How can a man know such as hearing the hearts' cry like we did?

There was the time spent in the study of the bible to prove that this miracle was not right. It was not of God! That was the main theme for about three weeks. As other things happened to reveal that Jesus wanted to work in the church some of the people had to figure it out. Everything was in question and the movement of God was hindered greatly. No one would say that anything was of Satan yet they tried to prove that it was not of God. How controversial can we get? Are there more than two forces in existence? Now everyone will agree that God stands alone in supernatural power but does he dare to use anyone that is not of the upper class, someone that is not in the click of that church. WE are our worse enemy Satan does not have to bother us at all. It is obvious that we can cause enough damage by just being left alone. Do you praise God for His interference? Think of it, if God did not interfere with us we would not even have the plan for salvation. Nor would we have the desire to love God back. In-so-much as while we were yet sinners Jesus died for us. Can we stop the pain that this causes in the church? I surely hope so!

Now please understand me. I am not claiming to be a prophet or some great big time MAN OF GOD or even some one special in any way. I am a man that loves our Lord very much, Father, Son and Holy Ghost! There is a true presence that all of God's children can enter into and the Lord can use any child like this for any of the gifts. We only need to be familiar with the scripture, always try the spirits and be obedient in most all things. Is this exceptional? Yes! What does it cost? Everything! You simply have to give up your wants to do what Jesus wants. It takes discipline, determination, dedication and love. If you can do the above efforts than you can glorify Jesus with all He wants you to do. Again prayer and fasting allows you to hear the Lord's voice and make sure what God ask of you, you can do. Here is my opinion of the greatest hindrance in God using anyone in any gift: not giving God the credit due him for the results. Do we fret when God decides to do things another way? Do we question the results when it does not go our way? Are we afraid of anyone not getting what they need? When its life and death can we just simply trust God? Can God use you? Will you think about it?

Here is a pain that we bring on ourselves since we do not understand all that God is doing in the church. It is the gift of the word of knowledge. Way too often can one say that if you weigh out the law of averages you must hit the mark quite often? This truly undermines the work of The Holy Spirit. Agreed, there are many taking advantage of this gift yet there are far more people that are following the leading of God. The main keys you can remember are; all words must line up with the scripture, you can not buy your healing, or a miracle and should never be persuaded to send money to get your needs met. The anointing is to lead all people to Jesus for healing, blessings, finances, and salvation and God only should be glorified and thanked for such as received from Him. When you release your faith in Jesus (not man) you can receive anything you need. If you want to send a little extra to support the ministry, that is between to you and God? Do not let people convince you otherwise! Your tithes and offering go to the local church that is there for you. If you receive your ministry from the TV and they are there for you; go to the hospital, visit your house, bring communion in or pray for you continually as a church would do, than you may ask God to send them your tithes and offerings. Other wise send a little extra if you wish but not out of anything but love.

In the church people really want to look good. There is something very special about being used of God in a very different way. When God does things that are not very common, people are identified with the Master and many receive treatment that they are not used to. It takes very little of this type of treatment to cause someone to want this constantly in their life. Our Lord does know our heart, mind and ability to handle different gifts on a full time bases. Normally what I see is that a gift is for the need at hand and then withdrawn to keep the praise and glory going to God. If we seek after this gift rather than God we loose all perspective of the normal. That is when we can fall into the traps of the devil without even noticing it. As we loose sight of God and can not hear His voice, then He has to send someone else to you to straighten you out. Also during this time God is using someone else to do the job He had intended for you. See what a mess we can get into without even trying very hard? When people go through this they can become very jealous of others God is using. That is when the pain comes in as they try to hurt those they are jealous of in the church. I do believe that this is the meaning behind the scripture that says, be led by the Spirit and you will not fulfill the lust of the flesh. Judgment, getting even, jealousy and envy can all cause us to do things that we should not. Let us get away from this pain and live in peace again.

There were many series of events that caused a tremendous amount of pain in the church. We seldom experience such unless you are on the top of your game with Jesus and Satan wants to break it up. At one point until now there was a large admiration for the youth to experiment with the mixing of races. Now do not judge me, my stand on this does not matter, what is important is how does the bible and society look at this issue? When it first began it was a huge battle field and many people got hurt on both sides of the line. My place was to be a peace maker and a minister of truth. The only reference I could understand was the mixing of believers and unbelievers. Yet our traditions really caused a huge uproar in the church. We had many blacks in our community that said such mixing was wrong and as many whites, Indians, Asians, ECT. On the other hand the kids could not see that it was a problem at all. Where do you draw a line? In the heart of every single individual that faces this question and has to deal with the loved ones involved. What is the answer? It is between the two people in the relationship. Our understanding of right and wrong does not supersede what God is doing in the hearts of others. When we leave it up to the one that can deal best with this answers cause the least amount of pain. Then actually happiness can come out of this subject. Jesus has the only true answers!

This we seldom faced yet it did come into the church every once and a while. When the power of The Holy Spirit would move on the music I believe that we need to let Him have his way. Normally without us hindering the movement there would be many needs met in that service. Most ministers yielded to the Spirit yet you would have a few that would try to steal our liberty in the Lord. They would insist that the preaching of the Word had to come forth every service no matter what else takes place. Some would bring this out in the way of testimony and would get people to think along the lines of preaching at all cost. This often brought question, doubt, fear, and unbelief. Needless to say that always quenched the Holy Spirit. With those emotions involved faith was hindered greatly. Then we might as well stop the service because Jesus could do no great works in our church. There was always a confrontation with said ministers and they would leave after they could not change me or the church. On the next service after they left, The Holy Spirit would move with such great power that He would leave everyone amazed. Yes, I was right but why did we have to face such pain and why not just let me minister freely?

We have had this feeling come into the church, slowly at first, that has over whelmed most ministers. There is this feeling that the trying of your faith is not to be revealed. Many statements that I have heard are that you never let anyone see you sweat. You act like everything is OK no matter what is going on. Now, part of that can have some value. I do not think you should ever let your guard down enough to be defeated. But the trying of your faith comes to show everyone that they can overcome just as you do. That is what allows your faith to grow, become strong and be a witness to others that they too can have a very strong faith in Jesus. We just can not give in and give up! For only through great faith can we see God move through us with the power that brings us to praise and worship the Lord for the great things He does. Until you overcome to the point of praise, you have not grown. You do not prove all He can do and through you He may not choose to move until you can show the victory. It would shock all of us to know how many people are struggling with this and what pain they may be in yet be too afraid of what people would think if it was revealed. Thank God for honesty in the church!

Still the greatest need in the church is truth. We must stop telling everyone that if they give their life to Christ that all your troubles are over. God's Word does not say that at all. Rather your trouble has just begun. Satan does not have you any more and he is up for the fight to get you back. He will pull out all the stops to try to cause you to give up. Pain should not come from the church yet when you surrender completely to Jesus that is where you will spend most of your time. What do you expect? The day he leaves you alone is when he has you again. Otherwise you are in for the fight of your life because that is what he does. Settle it in your mind that you must fight until you see Jesus face to face in heaven. Again your life of fighting should be filled with nothing but praise for all that Jesus brings you through. When your mouth is continually filled with praise and worship, then people will see something worth having. Then you can lead people to Jesus and expect Him to do just the same for them. Jesus does bless His children!

The hardest thing I have witnessed in any church I have ever been in is keeping hope alive. We make all kind of declarations and say all the right clichés. Stand on faith, fast and pray over the movement of God that he wants yet keeping hope alive is the hardest thing to accomplish in the Body of Christ. In the church that I pastured this too was the greatest pain we faced. Many a child of God just simply lost hope of God ever keeping the church moving on the right path. The excuse was man's sin, the reason was not trusting God enough to find the reason why we did not grow. Man would not have been accused, mocked, lied on and had rumors spread if they would have simply gone to work winning souls for Jesus. All these things begin to creep in when we get our eyes off of Jesus and His plan for building a church. Ninety nine percent of all pastors blame the congregation and ninety nine percent of the congregation blames the pastor. This game seems to allow Satan to subtly create every type of circumstance to attack the church until just the right thing divides and conquers. Our fault, OH yes, very much! Every member in the church is responsible for the church to follow the Lord in what He wants. When we stop winning souls we become too insensitive to keep each other out of trouble. Most of the ministries I have witnessed fall apart have been for the same reasons as above. Are we ever going to grow up in Jesus at least enough to see the devises of Satan before they can cause such pain? Well, I feel we had better the Lord is coming back soon. It is too late in time for us to be defeated, when hope dies do we ever have the faith in; others to do the right thing? Wake up church!

At one time there was a prophecy that revealed the wishes of God, that we would build a church for three hundred strong. Yet we moved into a building of about fifty seats and that would cramp us. Though the way we came about the building to rent so easily, we thought that this had to be the will of God. It was not to be our permanent home just a stepping- stone to the next place. However we shared this vision, it never took root. Too many knew more than God because the statement was said, (we can not fill up this building, why move on?) How often do we hear these statements and yield to them as wisdom? I am sure every mega church group of leaders has run into this statement over and over again. When are we going to learn that when God said it, He meant it? He will do His part, IF we do ours. Just simply do not stop winning souls for the kingdom. Do not get your eyes off Jesus. Stop being the judge of the universe and obey God. Do not fall for anything yet stop the pain! Realize that as imperfect as we are, God can deal with us sufficiently and bring us back to the right path. Of course that depends on our desire of serving Him and not ourselves. Please remember that every creature is worth saving or redeeming. If they can not be then that is God's place to give up on them, NOT OURS!

A great place to take on some of the best wisdom in the world is from your wife. Too many pastors do not realize why God put the two, man and woman, together. It was not only to fulfill your lust of a woman or a man (for you women pastors). The main purpose is to be the fulfillment of each other in every aspect of your lives. As well as being your conscience, protection from those that want to destroy what God is building in your marriage and church. When we fail to listen to God, many times our better half will hear Him and obey by telling what God wants. Many times they can hear the answer NO, when our minds often reject such. Most say, I'm standing and waiting on/in faith. God said, NO! Also ladies, God will never tell you to reach for sensual needs from your pastor. Just like men will never hear God say a lady pastor needs your emotional or sexual involvement in their marriage or ministry. Any help that draws another away from their spouse is SIN! This is also the job of the spouse to see, worn, and or stop, in the Name of Jesus. It is a shame that too many do not see this tactic coming from Satan and has the power in Christ to reveal and protect their partner. Even worst than that, is for anyone to think that God is sending another partner to help in their ministry. I do not care how you look at it; God gave you your spouse to aid your ministry and every aspect of your life. Anything else is lust and sin. Stay out of these messes and you will not fall. If you do not and fall, it may be for ever!

One lesson I believe that I have learned in the twenty years of ministry is that you must be sensitive to The Holy Spirit and determined to do what He tells you. Here in is one of the greatest failures of today. Just hearing the Lord is not enough. We must carry out the programs He sets in order, the way He directs. In the church we had a great hunger to hear God's voice. Yet, I do not know why we did not obey Him. The prophetic would come forth and there was one excuse after another not to obey. Over and over again I would warn the people that God may very well stop speaking because of this behavior. Though I could not get anything accomplished because there was always a way not to obey. It is my belief that if you do not do the little things that God wants, He will not give you the ability or power to accomplish the greater. If you are not going to witness to people, you fail the greatest commandment in the scriptures. Yes, we are to love the Lord our God above everything else but if we do not witness, we do not love Him to the fullest. If we do not live by the word that comes from his voice and the Holy Scriptures, we do not love him to the fullest. If we do not invite people to church, we are not convinced that God will meet them there so save their soul or meet their needs. We must obey and find purpose in service within the church.

Homosexuality was a cause of pain in the church. We reasoned with people that lived in this lifestyle to the point of pain and heartbreak. When two serious people came into the church wanting to be saved, our only instinct was to teach the scriptures and truth. They were two of the most sincere people I have ever met. When they could not get the results or proof of The Holy Spirit in their heart, they bombarded me with questions. I answered their questions as best as I could without compromise. As a result they said they were not sure they believed me. They did not see it that way. So the very next Sunday morning God gave me a message on Romans chapter two. Well, after the conviction of the Spirit got a hold of them, they both ended up in the alter praying. What really hurt me was that they believed they knew I preached the Word right and homosexuality was wrong. Yet their statement was, "that they would always live together and practice this sin openly." If they ever changed their way of living, I would be the first to know. They said not once did I condemn them and they could feel the love I had for them. This they never experienced in any church before. They would be back in due time. When will that time be? I do not know, yet I believe that it will happen before the end of time.

In this outreach of the church one young man really saw a means of victory in The Spirit. It was a hard lesson to learn and we seldom realize all the people that are impacted. It seemed that all the church entered into the prayer for deliverance of these two men, yet one young man particular. Too often he stated that people were repulsed by them and did not even try to help. None tried to understand their view of the emotional roller coaster ride they were on. At this time they had been together several years and had been to many different churches for help. Most all of them really blasted them without any concern for their feelings. Why must we go through the judgment of a church, without answers, they were torn down before they got the answers? This one man could not understand the reasoning of everyone wanting to hurt them. He knew the love given to him but why not just try to help without the pain? Do you realize how many people like this fall through the cracks of our churches without an effort? No we can not approve or condone the lifestyle yet, we can give truth without killing those that thought they wanted to hear such. His hearts cry was, they would get saved and change. Now at least he has the hope that they know the truth and can change.

Chapter Three

The Things Brought into the Church

Our hope in the Lord is to find someone that understands the many things that we go through. Many times we can not express this to anyone without the fear of it being transmitted all over town. When someone comes to the church, we must remember that we represent The Lord Jesus. The treatment of others will always be a great concern in the Father's heart. The bible talks about the bruises for our transgressions. I truly believe that this is relating to the pain we cause others. I have echoed this through out all my books and will echo it through out the world until Jesus comes back for us. It is time that the church stopped looking for new revelation long enough to see that we are creating far too much pain for others. One question, can this keep us out of Heaven? What is the scripture about becoming a stumbling block?

Truly I have tried to find one person that I could confide in and only my wife can fit the criteria. Imagine that? If this tends to ring home to you, it should convict you to be the person that others can depend on, be there and keep your mouth shut if they take a chance on you to confide in.

Many people say do not let the right hand know what the left hand is doing, as the scripture relates to in away of giving. This is a great thing and can benefit the giver every time as long as it is done not to draw attention. So many people can benefit through us just simply obeying God when He ask us to help someone. 3 John states that our charity should be spoken of to glorify God and as we do so, we do well. Please remember James: 3:10 humble yourself in the sight of the Lord and He will lift you up. You see if you try to lift up yourself in the sight of man than that will be all of your reward. It is much better to be rewarded by God, even if it is in secret! Again, I see a lot of teaching on being a partaker of whatever you may give under the anointing of the Lord. If it is healing than be healed. If it is finances than expect to receive the best to be returned to you. If it is deliverance than expect to be free from all that could bind you. Now, here is the greatest, if it is salvation that you are able to lead people into, expect the best gifts that God has to offer. Do not misunderstand me! The greatest gifts are not monetary, they are spiritual! These gifts when given away freely, will store up your treasures in heaven. Thus they will last forever and bring forth more fruit then you will ever know. There will be people coming up to you that you may have forgotten, that will witness your ministry to them and bless you far more that any gift you can receive other then salvation. This is what Jesus wants you to give and receive!

Seldom will a time pass in the church when there is no trouble what-so-ever. Yet there are times of refreshing when we can focus on just Jesus alone. What we often forget is that we can create these times with our worship. It is not a feeling, it is not an emotion, it is not a response to anything but it is deciding to lift up the name of Jesus no matter what is going on or what you are going through. Is it hard to do? YES! Very hard because Satan knows if we can get a hold of this we can constantly be praising the Lord and not get caught up in his devices. That is our victory and joy. I do believe that any time we can focus on Jesus instead of our problems then we are turning them over to Him and getting the promise of the Father. Casting all our cares upon Him for He care for us. Start with asking forgiveness, submission to God, correction, thanksgiving, and songs of praise until it becomes so dominate that we can enter worship. Let the tears flow and expect the peace that passes all understanding. You do not have to follow a pattern like this, do what it takes for you to get there (in the presence of God) and the victory will come every time! Praise His Holy Name, Jesus.

In a church that is hurting and struggling to obey God you will find it very difficult to stay under the anointing. For it is the anointing that breaks the yoke and we must operate under the knowledge that only God can give the anointing to reach hearts. No matter what the needs are without the anointing very few things happen. When this comes short, pray, repent and search the face of God with all you have within you. The anointing is the presence of God through the Holy Spirit in our hearts. Without a clean, obedient and humble spirit The Lord does not move much. Also it takes the Name of Jesus to accomplish anything. When God does not find the people acting right than He will work on us from the pastor to every one else. When He begins to use children to speak to us, then we know or should know, that we are is serious trouble. Sometimes God withdraws the anointing all together. Do not get in this shape! Keep your hearts clean and obedient! Humility will help you see deeper in the Spirit than you ever have before. Try it and see if I am right, it works for me.

We do not seem to learn lessons very fast in the body of Christ. I can not for the life of me figure out why some lessons are discerned and far away. Prayer and fasting seems to be the only way to really get through to the Lord and get anything through our hard heads. Many a church declares all the right things yet living in accordance is another matter. A tremendous pain that comes from this is judgment. Judging right from wrong is an absolute necessity. Yet judging people to be unworthy to be a part of your church is sin! Many a soul is setting at home, crushed because they were not worthy of any use in the church. Or to early placed in leadership and failed. Too often they were thrown away by the actions of those who tried to discipline them or simply whip them into shape. When are we going to learn that a child, no matter what age, needs teaching and encouragement because of what is to come at them?

Do not throw them to the lions before they are ready to close the lion's mouth. When are we going to learn that our mouth is the deadliest weapon a new Christian will ever encounter? Let me encourage each one reading this book. A beginner's class is very necessary if it is taught by one anointed to be an encourager and a worrier of prayer for the beginner. Great teaching and love creates in us great victories!

Have you ever heard the old statement, time heals all wounds? Well it is true. Much of the Church will learn a lesson in patience if they just simply allow God to work things out instead of taking things in our own hands. When we decide to handle things our egos often get in the way of truth and we fail to understand someone else's view. Usually that is when people get hurt the most and the healing process can be very long indeed. Example, why justify yourself? Normally only time will allow people to see you as you are when they will not believe you. So waiting on the Lord is the best defense because He will take up your cause as long as you are in the right. If you are wrong, be quick to repent, make it right and go on with Jesus. Heads up, stop giving Satan ammunition to destroy the church. Let us decide to work together, bless each other and be a blessing to God.

In the church we found great pain when it came to one seeing the sins of others. Too often we would see one confess their sin, publicly, and immediately someone would try to take advantage of them. Example, if someone was having marital problems there were always those around to hear every word, male and female alike. Then they seemed to have plenty of time to "witness" to them or their spouse. Other wise they did not have time to bother. Also when they found out that they could not take advantage of them, they would suddenly run out of time or became too busy to go on any farther. When will we learn that when a twenty or even thirty year old wants the attention of a fifty year old normally there should be a red flag go up. It would be wonderful if we could trust our lives with the people in the church but that is seldom the case. Some of the tale signs are, my spouse just does not understand, they just do not see me the way you do, it is easy to talk with you, and the spouse just does not give me enough attention. When these statements come at you, be careful. Some times there are no bad intentions at first but then it could be like taking fire into your breast. You are on the path to get burnt! We need to pray for a councilor that does not want to take advantage of us. Listen to God he will not fail you. Even an older pastor told us that God must have sent this woman to him. Wrong! God would never tell this man that he should leave his wife that had given him two children and supported his ministry for the last twenty years. He was taken captive by his lust.

Gifts are another way to get our focus off the individual and allow them to do things that are not right. Example; one person in the church was a very talented with paints. Professional was never in the question. Yet they did scenery that was quite good. In an innocent way he gave this picture to my wife and included me as a second thought. At the first look at the picture it seemed to be flawless. When we got it home, in the light, we could see the flaws. It was not all that good yet better then either of us could ever do. He never made a pass at my wife or anything like that but his alternative lifestyle started to show up. The Holy Spirit let me know that he was truly trying to get away from this. However it was a hard fight. I was sure the gift was to distract and it seemed so harmless. Much of our lives we will find this the case. When a thing seems innocent and yet we have this funny feeling about it that usually means something is wrong. We need to constantly try the spirits to see where they come from. All ministers want to be friends with the congregation and most of the time we can though we should never stop listening to the Lord as we make friends in the church.

Here was another problem that caused a lot of pain to me. There was a person that had a problem with drinking and went to several rehab programs. Each time he would come out he would return to the drink. It was devastating to his mother for years on end. Married with three children it was a great sacrifice for the family to endure the pain. Yet they kept trying to help not giving up on him. Constant prayer, fasting and seeking the Lord for every possibility, ended up draining them over several years that I knew the family. Shortly after they left the church there was a long term rehab program that he entered. When he came out of that he returned to the bottle again. I guess that was the last straw because a divorce followed and a tremendous heart-ache. At first we thought that he would commit suicide and we spent a tremendous amount of time in prayer. Slowly there were signs of him quieting the bottle. Even though he had broke so many hearts, even mine, there was always hope.

Yes, he did quit, joined a church in a larger city and seems to have a fair life. He keeps the children often and does a great job showing them his love. It is a shame that it was too late for their marriage but they all can make heaven by the life they are living now. Praise The Lord!

There is a prize that is more valuable than any amount of money, any accumulation of things, or any title one could ever have. It is greater than any power given by a job or any prestige all the fancy dinners offer. The prize is higher than the best seats and greater than the finest jewelry. Brighter then the sun, moon and stars combined. The most treasured possession in all the earth can only be peace in your heart, home, job, and church. It is one of the hardest fought battles that will never end but one worth whatever it takes to receive. The highest compliment received in our presence is the peace that anyone can feel when they are around us. Our reception of this has been none other than the love of Jesus in our lives, heart, and marriage. It was determined that we would not live fighting each other and by the grace of God, we have not! In every thing we try to do, we try to incorporate peace. You see that when the Lord told us that we could have the peace that passes all understanding, we believed Him. What a difference it makes when we are trying to make peace a priority. Love, true love, reveals in us the desire not to hurt the other at all cost. That alone will bring peace yet with the Lord's help it gets even better than that. As God is our witness it gets better as we go along and easier to come by. What a wonderful life God can give us if we just listen to Him! If we let God do this in our relationships that mean the most than job and church will have that peace that we bring into them.

There is another gift found in Jesus that every one needs on a daily bases. That is to find favor with the boss and all those that have authority over you. This gift comes with a very hard fought price as well. It is a hard thing to be in submission to those over you. We always are in the frame of mind that we should prove ourselves worthy of doing their jobs. "That is the way we get their jobs when they come open and we qualify through the other requirements." Yet in proving ourselves we become argumentative, sometimes bolder than we should and many times quite short with both our piers and management. In this state of mind we often find ourselves being left out of discussions, debates or even decision making. Even in the church we find many a pastor praying that certain ones do not show up because we know how they are going to act during a meeting. The favor with others first comes from God! If we are to behave right in His sight then the word tells us to do the same with any authority. Only when we do our job right, work hard and treat others right will we find favor with God and all authority. When we do not, it is not just our nature or the way we are, it is poor behavior that creates such pain. We need to change our behavior to become more like Christ!

God honors faith above most anything you can do except the relationship you have with Him. It is an absolute necessity that you keep your conversations and love constant with the Father. Also our faith must keep on the continual path of being exercised. One of the hardest discernments you will run into is the phony or fake. It is very difficult to see if one is working without a relationship with God, if all the right words, phrases, and cliques are in place. Many, if not all the time, God does honor ones faith that is asking for a need being met. Here even if the anointing is not upon the minister, it will appear to be because the blessing still comes. God really can work things out in a sovereign way when we think he is going through someone. Where do we draw the line? Well that is between you and God. We are such poor judges of people we often hurt God's work yet ones lifestyle must add up to the scriptures. Another way of expressing it is to line up with the scriptures. We are not always perfect but we can always be clean in God's sight. It is something we must work on daily with the help of our conversations and again love with the Father. We do not have to be sin friendly, a phony, or a fake. We can surely be a child of God through the Blood sacrifice of Jesus and the presence of the Holy Spirit in our heart. That is relationship!

There is something that I have found that all ministers have trouble getting the churches to receive. That is focus! If we ever get a hold of this precious gift we can truly move mountains. Too much of our prayer life is spent chasing rainbows across the sky. We often start out right but are soon shifted into a different area and loss focus completely. How many times have you gone to the Lord in prayer for one person and within seconds of the prayer you are bombarded with twenty other names? What happened to praying for one until you was released by the Lord to move on to the next? Do you imagine that that is why you are not praying through until you get results? The Word tells us that the house of God is to be, "a house of prayer" yet are we effective? You can not drive a car frontwards by looking backwards at the same time. You will hit something! Our focus in prayer is the same way. We have to overcome confusion and clutter to get into focus with the Lord. I dare to go as far as this may be the reason we do not hear the still small voice of the Holy Spirit in times of great need. We can not see our intentions, motives, and needs clearly enough to find the right way to pray. If we could focus, God would teach us to overcome this and any problem that would distract our prayer life. This is the difference in one who prays and a prayer warrior.

In the same measure let us look at the double-minded person. I will support your ministry with my time, prayers, presence, and attendance to the church services. Then you never see them again. Did God change His mind? Was they mistaken? Did they fail to see the future for themselves and needs of their family that would have been met in our church? No, no and yes. Their mind was right to come to us yet their obedience failed. The stability was lost when they decided to disobey God and left them double-minded. Another example; a lady told me seriously that the Lord told her if she would come to our church that her son would be healed. I have related to this story before in the book but it fits this teaching perfectly. Well, I was never told why they did not showed up but their son is still in a wheelchair and his mind is the same. God did not change his mind toward this precious family. He seriously wanted to bless them with a miracle because after her call He dealt with my faith until I was ready to do His will. Again you could be delivered from your drinking if you would just simply give your heart to Jesus and get involved in a church for support. I know that is what God told you because He told me too. He wanted to be free but did not want to surrender just yet. The bible says that a double-minded person should not even think that they will receive anything from God. Why are we like this? Can we change? Yes! We better.

In the fulfillment of righteousness we have as many doctrines as we have people. Yet the commandment is still there and we should do all we can to fulfill God's commands. When John the Baptist baptized Jesus we find the completion of righteousness in the law. Jesus did what was right he did not reject or change that command of God. Therefore it is our privilege to complete the act of love by the baptism of water. As this act is in the heart so it is in the kingdom of God, do not get hung up on the differences just follow the leading of the Holy Ghost and you will be alright. I have seen too much pain in the church over water baptism and it is time that we just simply allowed God to interpret the scripture and stop hurting people. Do you agree?

One of the greatest problems I believe that we have faced in any church is that of discouragement. It is very difficult to deal with other's problems while you are beat down and no one is trying to help. Many a day went by for me and other ministers that I have talked to when we wondered if there was any one that cared for the preachers. We spend the majority of our time alone with The Lord and yet we still need that time with people to talk things out. The only ones that came my way seemed to want to take advantage of the situation to make their self look good. So too often they spread the fear or failure all over the place. The next thing you know is the whole church is not only discouraged but ready to quit. The statements that came back to me and other preachers that I talked to were; well if you can not do this how do you expect us to, if you do not think our time is accomplishing anything, why continue, if there is no hope for us, let us just quit, well, I guess that if you are not good enough give up, or even worse, just let us find some one else we will listen to them. Sometimes this statement is right it is time to move on without putting the blame anywhere. But most of the time I have found that we need to fast and pray. Get back to our first love and seek the face of the head of the church, Jesus until we can hear from heaven and know what to do with the church. Then through repentance we can find our way back to the right track and listen to the point of obeying the word of truth. Hope will return and you will be ready for revival to break out again.

Too often there is this feeling that a little lie is OK. When you look into the church you would not think such would be acceptable. Yet today it seems there is so much of the world involved in the church that it is just a part of everyday behavior. Our Lord made it very clear that all liars will find their place in hell. Now my question to you is did He mean it? When a witch hunt is wrong, when an accusation is false, when one is defamed, when one is disrespected, when one fails to achieve even though they tried, when one is called on the carpet for not obeying man and standing on what God had said, are these the little white lies that we think we are going to get away with since we are in charge? I really believe that there will be many a sorrowful heart when we try to explain such to Jesus face to face. Or do you think that when we see Him we will know that there would be no excuse or attempt to cover it up because of popularity? Where I stand or lay on my face before God is in the now. Let us get it right! Let us admit the wrong, repent turn away from it. Most important let us stop hurting so many of God's children with lies.

It gets very difficult to deal with the inner most parts of the heart and to put that in writing for others to read is rough. There is a feeling of opening yourself up to more pain than you have already experienced. When it seems like everyone wants to tear down any ministry we find it difficult to find help. I have found great relief in writing and reading the experiences again. This has been so rewarding to look at a problem from (almost) a different view. Like the expression, "what would Jesus do?" As I view it this way there is a greater awareness of a deeper meaning. The whole picture of what God is or was doing seems to come alive and it's easier to accept, forgive or ask forgiveness. This has been my blessing and it looks like I will be writing for the rest of my life. Praise God!

Many people make up the church of today and yesterday's church was made up of many of their parents. This is the importance of keeping your children in church. It is not just the revealing of Jesus but the morals, character, and disciplines needed in society. Our success is determined by our relationship with Jesus and also the world all around us. To cut either out would be to the failure of any church. Our constitution declares a separation between, the church and state yet never would it have been the intentions of our forefathers to leave these factors out of our teachings. God was the purpose of the founding of the new world called, The United States. He still is whether we agree or not. Our children are being bombarded with all the education available and that is a good thing, yet do not leave out God from your teachings. The joy and victory in the revelation of Jesus will take our children through this life with a sense of belonging and purpose that can not be found in any other way.

One of the greater problems in the church was to see a man different than he can be. We have this preconceived idea that there are perfect people in the world that can never make a mistake. Too often these ideas are backed up by very carefully stated comments such as; if he was truly under the anointing than he would not be in the wrong or he would not say anything wrong. Well we are human and even though we have no intentions of making mistakes there is always that possibility. I hear constantly a minister say I made a mistake once. That does make one think that there should not be any made while preaching. What we fail to realize is that everyone takes things very different. How can we make a comparison to events that happened two thousand years ago with modern language without some people getting confused? I have never heard a perfect sermon even when it was read from paper or someone's notebook. What a shame it must be for

God to look down from heaven and see all this needless judgment going on.

Here is one of the strongest problems in every church that I have visited. We truly do not get a hold of the Word without finding ourselves focused on the preacher or teacher bringing the Word. It is so hard not to pay attention to the one speaking and not hearing what God has to say. We tear apart the delivery, word usage and the jesters expressed. Is.55:11 told us that before God has one of his messengers bring the Word God has sent it to get the job done. Whether it is salvation, deliverance or healing, God has already anointed the Word with the Holy Ghost to give us what we truly need. When we get our eyes off the messenger and on the Word speaking, then we will see much more of the signs and wonders promised. I believe that we will not hurt so many preachers if we just simply follow these methods of discipleship. Pray to study, listen to the Word and take your eyes off the messenger. Remember God's Word will save, deliver and heal, not God's man. Through the name of Jesus will all man be saved, let's focus on Jesus and we will get a lot more out of the ministry and ministers.

We constantly find ourselves trying to explain a denomination that we do not belong to and do not truly understand all that they teach. I have often wondered how we get so much information and how we understand word usage when it is truly different from our own. Many an occasion I have found myself listening to another explain what others believe and wonder if it was accurate. Sadly in talking with ministers of that denomination I have found the facts turned around completely. What a shame! Do we have to defend what we believe? Or are we just trying to prove someone else wrong? Is this important enough for us to spend any of our precious preaching time? After all, I have heard that there are people that we may only get one chance to reach them with the good news about salvation. If this is true let us use our time wisely. Why not find these answers on our own by using the people who could tell us the truth? Then take this out of our church to teach true doctrine. Think about this and see what you feel?

I have found in all churches that I have been in many a soul that is seeking a position of recognition. This usually can cause a great pain in the church as people play politics or have this wish to serve and do not do the work. When one fills the slot they are the only one that has any say over this area in the church. Most pastors keep an eye out for just this type of problem but I have seen it get by them. Then many a time if the suggestions do not come from them, they reject all. Without realizing that this can happen we find a monster in the church and no one working where God has ordained a position. If this is seen too often it is either ignored or there is a great rip in the church to straighten it out. To eliminate this type of problem I believe that each position should be under a trial period to see if they are going to do the job.

If they are not, then explain it and remove them. If they do the job then encourage them, help them and strengthen their efforts.

Chapter Four

God Will Take You Only as far as You Want to Go

Good things come to those who wait! This is a statement I thought was for someone else and never meant for me. Yet God's Word is never to return to him void. So there is something missed when his word does not work for you. We want to search everyone's closet but our own. Why is that? It is so meaningful to each of us to have a talking relationship with God so why not admit the things that are wrong? How hard is that? Well I believe that the answer is found in those who are anointed and those who are deeply anointed. The difference is as night and day. We must get back to the understanding that God knows all things open or secret so just confess. Then the Lord can get on with the intentions of taking us further then we have ever been. When we get the basics down we can go on to the blessings. If we fail the basics, we should not expect the blessings. It is like if this spirit scares you do not expect God to reveal a stronger one. You can not handle it and God knows not to put you there.

In our little church we found people that wanted to get very deep into the word yet did not want to do the work unless it was convenient for them. Or it was their project, idea or one of their family's, than they were all into it. It would always seem that they did not want the attention yet if they did not have it mentioned from the pulpit they would bring it up. I had trouble understanding the difference because when the recognition was not given it would be a long time before anything else would be brought up. In trying to explain this to the new converts it became very hard for them to believe that this was not the way to go. You see the example you set or allow is the way they learn right from wrong. Even when they are listening to the word preached. Your life is what people believe the most so you must be very careful in how things are presented in the church. There again the cause for pain just slips in as a double standard. All my life and ministry I have heard the question. "They can be this way but I can not?" How difficult it must be for one to realize that some people are excused from bad behavior and others are reprimanded. Then you preach from the pulpit it is wrong. Do you see why new Christians have such a hard time getting started on the right foot? It is not just family that gets this special treatment. Sometimes it is the tithes, popularity or friendship that is treated with a double standard. This is simply wrong even if no sin has been committed because of the example that it sets before the new Christians. What is that scripture that states we should abstain from the very appearance of evil?

In our old church as well as any other church we tried to set an example of what is right and wrong. It is not only by our words but our actions, in and outside the church that will make a difference. This standard is very hard to maintain on a continual bases. Yet we feel we must try to do what is right all the time. What is so precious to us is that our Lord does understand these efforts and blesses every attempt. This keeps it from becoming a burden but a pleasure because we know that it pleases Jesus so much. The efforts of being right will not grieve the Holy Spirit and this makes it a fun relationship. This makes the partnership the main focus. Look at the old covenants and you will see that both parties had a roll to play in the agreement. Our roll is to love Jesus so much that we do not ever want to hurt The Trinity in any way. This allows us to have a good time with God and enjoy the trip as we pass through this life. Depression, turmoil and many a heart ache becomes from too hard a lifestyle. We just can not seem to make it right. Well, I say learn to enjoy your relationship with God and it will not be too hard. You can make it right by ENJOYING Jesus' company and pleasing him.

I feel that there is a deeper meaning to discipleship than most people ever receive from the Lord. We have too many ideas of our own to listen. So the parable that Jesus taught is really true. We want people to look up to us in every area of our life and this causes us to error in our teaching. The word that I receive is that the child should be taught salvation first and then be taught how to be as free from sin and this world as Jesus was. Our greatest fear is that if people see us as we are then there can be no way they will follow us. Here is where we need to make up our mind as a teacher or preacher. Are we drawing people to us or are we leading people to Jesus? Tough words are they not? Yet people needs to see that we are real and not some phony that can not make it to heaven. People, the only way we are going to make it will be to follow the Holy Spirit all the way there. Saved by the grace of God through the shed blood of Jesus on the cross of Calvary and filled with the Spirit to lead the way. Our job is to lead/ disciple people to Jesus and show every one the joy of salvation by living with The Lord.

One of the things that troubled the church of yesterday and still a problem today is anger. This has become a problem that has overwhelmed most everyone and every person that tries to follow Jesus. We can not speak with surety that this is the problem of everyone but it sure has been a complete nuisance in the church. More and more we find that there is this conflict of the leaders as well as with the people in the church. Too often we find that there is not a peaceful solution to anything. When are we going to wake up? We do not see that it is normal "when we see that we can not do what we want," get angry, mad or in rebellion? Some one stops us from what we want and immediately we attack. We can not see that normally when this happens it is for our own good. God says no because it is going to hurt, kill or destroy us or some one else. Too often we do not realize it is God saying no when the pastor stops different things in the church. We want, we think, we know or we say! When are we going to realize that we do not have to hurt anyone if they just simply learn that Jesus is suppose to be in charge not us? When Jesus steps into a church peace rules and every one that is of God loves it that way.

Too often I have found my failures and the pain of others to be the results of not being able to do as I want. Or with others their way was not the way that God was leading so we could not accomplish the goals we were trying to reach. In that came discussed, discouragement and many times fighting within the church. Rather than yielding to the Holy Spirit we would find ourselves trying to prove that we had the right answer. This always brought strife and blindness to the children of God so as we could not easily see how to solve the problems. Sometimes pride entered in, other times the pecking order took hold and yet others were just caught up in anger. Too often people ended up leaving the church with hurts that went very deep. Why not solve the problems rather than letting the devil overtake us? Here is a great rule of thumb that I believe that God has given us, if there is not peace in the church about any project, do not do it. I have found that there are always those that would not agree to anything yet the true children of God will find their solutions this way.

We are being bombarded with the sin friendly church that will crowd its way into different aspects of the church. Never will it come in like a flood but little hints of the possibility of being right. First it was the hint, then the argument. What does the bible really mean? Did it really say this? Do you not think it is outdated?

How can it apply to today? When these questions start popping up I automatically see a red flag and know that something bad is trying to get into the church. Listen, I feel that we do not talk enough about the wages of sin. Can we without the shed blood of Jesus reach heaven? Will the sin we commit in this life create a problem for us even after we are saved? The answers to these questions are both yes! Sin has a way to distort the way we think and look at any part of life. It is much easier to accept something wrong and we find that our common since is totally lost. Sin opens the door to allow anything else to slip in, like a lie, a cover up, an excuse or even the attempt to get others involved. We try to follow The Holy Spirit in this condition and find that He is only going to lead us to repentance. On top of all this we will find that sin brings sickness, disease and even death. These lessons are going to be brought out in greater details in the chapters to come.

Be not deceived God is not mocked if you sow to the flesh you will reap destruction. If you sow to the Spirit you will reap life and that everlasting. As I got older and my body started to give me a lot more trouble health wise, I find myself paying more attention to the scriptures on healing. In our life time it is evident that the sin has an effect on our health. We do abuse ourselves way to much and expect our health to be good. Well, I am of the opinion that you pay for your abuse even though Jesus has forgiven you of your sins. We seldom get into good physical shape overnight and we can seldom get into better shape instantly. It takes work and I know that Jesus can help us learn how to better treat ourselves.

At one point I was at the place of heart failure but God intervened and by listening to The Holy Spirit I have come a long way. Yet it has taken a lot of work, prayer and obedience over the last several years.

The good health came from Jesus and the maintenance had to come from my working on better care. Keeping from the sin that can abuse my body and working in better ways to be healthier. Praise God for second, third and even more chances for some of us! Amen?

I believe that being healthy can keep disease away. Our system was made to defend from anything that can come against us and God intended for us not to get sick. Yet he also intended for us to take care of ourselves to keep our immune system in the best shape it could be. The sin of neglect or abuse tears down that defense allowing disease to attack. Then instead of being on defense we end up on offence. Our first response should be to find the abuse or neglect and straighten that out. Then go to the Lord to straighten out the disease or sickness that came into our body. Yet I have found that this can be a process and a painful one to learn. By not learning the right way of care we often end up repeating that mistake over and over again. Why is it so hard to understand that you dress according to the weather? You do not get too hot or too cold. You can even eat in the right manner for the weather and it will help. Now do not ask me for your diet but I know that it works according to God's plan for your life.

Another great aspect of our health most would not even agree to unless they have seen the results. This is to be careful of the company you keep. We never want to shun anyone and I have only seen a few people that I just do not go around. It is because of their influence in certain areas that cause such trouble. They do not just have to be dreadful sinners to aim you in the wrong direction. A negative influence on things you are trying to get control of will hinder your faith and even bother your trust in God's ability to help you. Even as strong as that is the concept of you not being good enough for God to help. How many times have you heard people say that some things you have to do on your own? I am sorry this is the type of area or presence you need to stay away from in order to get the help you need. It is my belief that God is interested in every area of your life and he wants to be a part of all you go through especially the painful parts. So sickness, disease and every ache and pain is important to our Lord. That is how great his love can be for all of us! Trust him and let him guide you through anything that is hindering your health and know it is important to Jesus.

Today I feel that the fear of the Lord has revealed a generation that begun their fall back ten years ago. Many a prophet stated the fear of this happening and it seemed like it fell on death ears. I feel like a lot of prophecy has had the same end as those did. It is a shame to look back and question why did we not listen? Will we hear the next group of prophecy listing the end of time and the final revival? We see the falling away of respect for the authorities set up by God. There is also a great loss of care for the elders and the disadvantaged. It is my feelings that this is leading up to the last days where our

Lord will get tired of us hurting each other and put a stop to it. The tremendous anointing coming upon the men/women of God that will stand up for those that are treated wrong has already begun. There is a power that has come forth that will stop the witch hunts and false accusations yet the blame game will continue until the end has come. The future will be swamped with the kind of teachers that will love the expressions of how good they make people feel. Not the much needed conviction of sin. This started in our church when people got tired of the ministry of reaching souls and the visible lives changed. Will we listen to the prophecy of today or will the future catch us asleep and asking why we did not know that this was going to happen?

Our church of yesterday was built on the wonderful faith in Jesus as his saving grace, deliverance and healing came forth like water. It seems like we should never get too much of the experiences of this glorious presence. Yet in time man has always proven that good rules it can only last for so long. It is to our shame that we get weary of doing and seeing God move by his Spirit. The feelings of the music and the excitement of the dance should be allowed forever. Yet when the power comes to change lives we only allow so much before we rebel. Part of that is from the double standards and yet another side is that we like to live the way we are. It is sad that when it is your child doing wrong people will climb all over them. But when it is their child, well God understands. Again when God is trying to get us to move into a cleaner lifestyle we just can not seem to get there. If the preaching gets too hard the expression is we need to lighten up because no one can really live that close to perfect. Can we really believe that God can look upon the Blood of Jesus and accept us without us changing at all? Then why should we study to show that we have improved?

This really needs to be studied out because our soul really does depend upon our walk with Jesus. Where do we draw the line of compromise at the beginning or the end?

Now let us get down to a very personal level of pain that many would not talk about. Mainly because they do not want to admit that the problem could exist in their life. We are constantly expressing how we want to follow Jesus in every way yet when it comes right down to it we want to go our own way instead. Yes we say the right words and say the right prayers but we look for the solutions within our intellect and the experiences that we have been through. Even if we have failed over and over again we will still look for it to work this time. What is really hard is that when we go to our self instead God we find other sins slip in easily. If any battle gets into an all night course of loosing the fight then we better go back and see where we left Jesus. As we find him and submit to his path he will once again protect and defend off the attack by giving us enough of the word to win. This attack could be sex, money, power or anything that would come between us and God. I will never say that the battles are not hard but if they last more than a few minutes, no lest hours, you should go looking for where you left Jesus. We do need him every minute and every hour of every day.

Seeking the perfect will of God has been a life long adventure that never seems to cease or ever stop. It is our joy to express our love for Jesus by our obedience! We must keep our efforts alive and alert ever seeking to please him and also knowing that this effort will be rewarded with the power that glorifies Jesus continually. When these goals are set on the back burner we find sin in the camp and pain in the heart, ours or some one else. There is too much time spent on our getting attention from others or even God in ways that are not right. When you seek attention many times we find our focus on ourselves instead of Jesus. Here is where anything could slip in with little discernment. When we seek Jesus' face we do the things that are pleasing to him like helping others or just simply talking to him and waiting for him to answer. Seeking his love will bring you into a point of praise and take you to a place of worship. This is the greatest place in all of existence because here is where you stop asking for things and just simply want to know him. Believe me this is what Jesus wants the most! He does love to bless us and will continually yet it is the relationship that is the most important.

The greatest joy that I think I have is to lead someone into the presence of Jesus in praise and worship. There is no way to do this without going into this praise yourself. That is where the greatest blessings lie and where I want to be all the time. As any one could see we do not have to be a great singer or fabulous music leader with all the school we could get. Please do not take this wrong! Get all the school you can because it will truly help. Yet the point I am making is that it is a matter of the heart not the perfection of the arts. When I wish to really get into the Lord, it is praise where I start and finish. It does not take but a moment for Jesus to get involved in praising the Father. Then The Holy Spirit really takes us into a deeper presence than we have experienced before. Yes I believe that each time you worship you can go deeper and deeper. I do not like the expression of different levels yet there is a closeness that can not be denied. I do not want levels of love it is my desire to have a presence that tells me Jesus is so close that his voice should be expected. Then I can receive with open arms and mind his will and purpose for my life.

There has been many a soul that has come to me with a dissatisfaction of their life not reaching their potential. This is a tool of the devil that hinders most people I know. We allow this tool to keep us from true worship and praise whether we are sick or not. Our hearts are the main theme that takes us into the presence of God and when that is not where it should be we come up lacking. In ourselves we do not necessarily see the problem slipping in yet when we try real hard to find Jesus, he is there but we are not. Somehow we just can not get where we need to be and it is not always easy to detect the problem. It is like when we confront an evil person in demon possession, all the minor spirits seem to be revealed first to throw us off the main spirit in control. When he is revealed the battle is short and victorious in Jesus' Name. As a major spirit is cast out, the rest follow suit, without a fight. The reason is that they do not hold the power to stay. There is the same barrier in the heart when our lives do not reach the mark that we think it aught to and we fail to get close enough for this to be revealed. This tells me that the need of being able to listen is just as important as being able to express our heart. Do you agree? Remember talk and listen to Jesus.

Our ministry has been wide open for many a year with no fear of what God has asked of us. Yet often we find that for any one to just simply say that this is my ministry from Jesus is hard. Too often when you reveal this every one seems to start taking pot shots at you. Mainly just to put you down or try to see if what you say is true. The older I get the more senseless this becomes. Why do we spend so much energy trying to destroy any ministry? Well never the less, my ministry has been deliverance from day one and over twenty years of great joy seeing people being set free. Each church that I have entered The Lord has revealed this and the attacks begin. I am not always sure that the revelation is so important but I do know that after this comes out many people find their selves seeking help. When a heart starts seeking after what is right in the sight of God they find him quickly. That is when he really comes alive on their behalf. Most deliverance is rapid and easy to receive. Yet keeping clean is the hardest part. When we learn how to stay close to Jesus all the time we will learn how to keep our deliverance, healing or salvation.

A beautiful event took place that reminded me of the many times Jesus tried to reveal how simple it is to worship and how important it is to us. We have a Yorkshire that is three years old and we spend a lot of times pampering her. She in return has given us so much unconditional love that it has been really wonderful. Yet she is totally dependent upon us for most all of her needs. Bathing, feeding and the giving of attention are just a few things that take place since she has moved in here. The other morning she had ate her breakfast with me and left the kitchen. Not hearing anything I assumed that she went back to bed which was her custom. When I went back through the middle room she was laying in the floor balled up in a fettle position. She does lie this way some but there was something wrong and she was not making a sound. With her eyes open I knew it was not fatal but wrong. Checking her out I found that her hind paw nail was stuck in her whiskers and she could not get loose. After it seemed funny but at the time I was concerned. With just a little effort and not a bit of pain I loosed her completely. Boy did she get excited spinning in circles jumping upon me licking and dancing like this was the greatest thing that had ever happened to her. It reminded me of how I felt the first time I surrendered my heart to Jesus and how free I felt from the sin that had me bound. The excitement overwhelmed me and on every thought of it still sends me into a state of extreme joy and happiness. We could take a great lesson from this and release ourselves to the freedom of worship without any reservations. Truly this would be what Jesus wants from all of us. It really made me feel good when our puppy showed that much appreciation, can you imagine how God would feel if we showed him that much?

I know that there are as many ways to worship God as there are people in the world today. And I feel that decency is the only real requirement from him. I can not believe that anything vulgar or sexual would be accepted but other than that Jesus loves the expression of worship. Now not everyone has to express their selves the same and I am sure that the Lord enjoys the variations of the heart. To me the key is the expression of the heart in love showing the Greatness of God and our appreciation of him being in our lives. His presence causes me to want to praise to the point of worship and continue always to keep him close to me. He does live in the presence of praise and I enjoy ever minute that can be spared to show him how much I want him there with me. Continually I want to praise him in all my actions and interactions with others. This is where miracles come from and healings seem to be the order of the day. What a great joy we have for the God of all creation living in our hearts and being ever aware of this miracle. If you are not expressing your praise and worship to Jesus then it is time to begin, it is never too late to show how much you love him.

There are many hurts in the church that gets reviewed by the sinners. Too often these pains keep people out of the church because they do not want to be a part of such. We as part of the church tend to cause both sinner and saint alike to stay away. One such thing that we do is to bash other churches. Too often we feel it is our duty to reveal the faults of others in order to explain the benefits of our church. This is where we get into trouble. Normally we do not know what the other churches teach or lead others by and yet we feel that we can be an authority because we talked to someone in that church. Listen if a person is not living for Jesus then they find every excuse under the sun to keep from going to a church and find what is wrong in their life. If you talk to enough of these people in this condition you will find that they all find the same faults. With those faults they are armed with excuses to combat any conviction of going to another church where they could find Jesus. As children of God we can not give them any more ammunition against their or any other church to keep from getting right with God. We need to learn that bashing the church only causes a greater falling away. On top of that as we realize that churches are made up of you and me then we can see that they are all imperfect. Yet they are all trying to help people to get to God through the blood shed on Calvary. If they are not teaching this, than we need to turn them over to God but leave them alone. Bashing them will never change them or normally help anyone else to find Jesus. Every child of God should find the meaning of stumbling block and see if we are taking part in that action.

In any church we will find that we will have trouble with certain ways of understanding what is being taught. Some preachers are very good with their expressions and descriptions of the many words used in that area of the church. Others really struggle to get across what they believe. One such tool is confusion and the devil knows how to use it well to keep a fuss going. Even the deepest anointed ministers find that someone took something they said wrong and have a problem with such. This is a daily battle in all churches that I know and one that will not soon go away. We must learn where to find our answers rather that to tear down the pastor outside the church. Why is it that we have to prove every body wrong and that we are right? Who are we in Christ? Are we a child or a judge? Most will say I am not judging I am just trying to find the truth. Well then why all the arguments with so many people outside the church? Why the fuss in the church? Can we trust the preachers any more? Can we trust the good intensions of man? Are we so far away from God that he can no longer explain the meaning of the scriptures and help others also? We must get right with God and become a help in the church not a killer with the tongue.

Hard words are they? Well sometimes I have found that people do not mind using hard words against others but do not want them coming back to themselves. When the time comes that the church would rather have a goose bump than the truth then it is time to wake up the sleeping giant and shake up the soul to receive from God. My ministry has been that of a very soft, gentle man. Only a shouter when the Holy Spirit really gets me excited and begins to work miracles. In order for me to become what God wants me to be I must start revealing those things which are hard to receive. I have always thought that I have given the message just as he gave it to me and feel now that he is changing the method because of the way people are responding. For anyone to follow the Holy Spirit we must realize that the message does not change but when hearts start to harden then it takes something extra for him to get through. Our good time messages are still going to come through and prosperity is real today yet we must start hitting home to help people realize the pain they are creating either on purpose or accidentally. It is time to stop it and help people without such horrible scares that last a life time.

It is a hard thing to realize that people get tired of walking in the Spirit and can not seem to continue very long without a rest. It is our desire most of the time for a deeper anointing through a closer walk with Jesus though we seldom realize exactly what that will cost us. Our interaction with others will dictate to us the response of God in that desire. Even if we realize how difficult that could be we do not always try to correct ourselves. This causes God to have to deal with us because of the pain we cause others. Will we ever learn this simple lesson? I am truly not sure. I have been teaching this for twenty years and the body still has not caught on. Most of my family still fights this same battle over and over to the point that it seems daily. When doing right and doing good seems to be too hard you would think that we would want to stay in the Spirit continually. Why not? Are the pleasures of this life so important? What is the greatest hindrance to you? I know in myself that Jesus made this very clear when he said that we was first loved by God in order to love him. There has to be a certain draw that keeps that relationship (closeness) alive. This is where the Holy Spirit comes in to keep us in a state of joy and happiness walking with Jesus daily. Our lack of walking with God is one of our greatest failures that causes hurt in so many others. Because when we are not close to God we are not as sensitive to others feelings as we should be. Think about it!

Chapter Five

Doing the Right Thing Brings Good Decisions

Let us look at another area that seems to be constantly in the view of all churches in the world today and was here yesterday. Open your eyes to the reality of decision making and try to realize how many times you have seen this occur. Without the feeling to fast or pray most churches will decide to do a certain project and pray for God to bless. These decisions normally come with a great deal of controversy and a great division in those that agree or disagree. Too often there is this feeling of division and we ended up with another sinful split in the church. We must realize that division does not come from God. It is not a way to reveal the spiritual or those that should be in charge. When we can not agree on anything we should wait on the Lord to bring every one around to where they could hear from God and know his will. Or we need to let the leaders take control and solve the problem. I have made the comment over and over again and feel like it should be recognized as valid for all things pertaining to the church, constantly it is the blind that always want to lead. We must avoid this and spare the souls of the blind. Who are the blind? Look at those that are constantly coming up with the ideas that never work or cause a great deal of pain for others.

In every church there are those that know what is best and will prove it at all cost or pain to anyone. Our church was no different and if a certain person was not involved no one else would be. This normally caused a lack of growth and a visual show to the community that the church was controlled by this one. Here was where many people stated to me that there was nothing they could do in the church. So why come? Most churches that I have been in had the same problem and seems like no one could overcome. When every one stopped trying to change that then we sat still and stagnated. The anointing was always there yet not every time people would get in and enjoy the presence of the Lord. Here we are several years later and I am finding the same thing hindering the movement of the Holy Spirit in the services. When are we going to get out of the normal services and let Jesus have his way in our heart? Because you see it is the heart that has to be reached in order for us to truly worship the Lord our God and Savior Jesus Christ.

I know that I have touched on this before and will touch on it again. Yet there is an opening that has come into the churches that will cause a lot of people to fall if this is not confronted. Once we have tasted of the will of

God through the saving grace of the shed blood of Jesus and have had the presence of the Holy Ghost in our heart so we can not return to the letter of the law! We can not deny Jesus to look for his coming as the Jews do today. We can not return to the letter of the law for it kills! The law was brought forth by God to reveal Jesus and the coming sacrifice of sin. As Jesus fulfilled the blood atonement that was all that could ever be done to have a relationship with God. We must accept Jesus' sacrifice for our sins and make him Lord of our lives. That is the meaning of salvation! Anything else will dispute the effect of the finished work of Jesus. So do not fall into that trap of Satan and overcome by the blood of Jesus and the word of our testimony.

Our freedom in Jesus does not allow us to willfully sin this will remove the Holy Spirit from our lives. Not by his choice but by ours. We purpose in our heart to lust and that we want to commit sin in order to drive the Spirit out. Maybe we do not word it that way but every time we willfully sin that is exactly what we do. You see it is the Spirit that brings the Word of God alive so we can see sin. As we walk in the Spirit we find the strength to overcome this world and the pain therein. You will then become victorious children of the most high God and joint heirs with Jesus of everlasting life. In this state of being we find the anointing flow through us as water miracles, healings and salvation is the order for everyday. When will we learn that all doctrines are not of God? There are many false teachers and preacher out there that are trying to get a following and if we are not careful we too could fall. With these goals in mind they tend to bring in a new thing or revelation that no one else has ever picked up on. Then they make disciples after themselves and not Jesus. Wolves in sheep's clothing they are. Beware!

When any church opens up to their faults there should be changes that would lead them to a very productive ministry. Too often they can not see their faults or refuse to change and continually remain closed minded to the changes God wants. We can not be led by the Holy Spirit with a closed mind. Too often our preconceived ideas will not allow us room for anything different. Some habits are great when it becomes prayer, fasting, helping others and always looking for lost souls. Yet we get into this rut of doing the same o same o and accomplish way too little in our ministry. I do not believe that it is time for a new thing in ministry. I believe that it is time that we reached more people for God by getting out and talking to people. We are way too closed up in our little houses and way too comfortable to make a difference in our community. It is not enough for people to look across the street and see you do the right thing. That is good but how will they know the motive of God's love unless they hear it from your voice. Most of our neighbors will tell others of the fights, arguments, and turmoil that have gone on. Why is the love of God hidden? If we begin to spread the Word of God in our community it will be productive in the church.

The Sweet Holy Spirit has continually brought back to my mind the things that we have dealt with in the church. One such thing was the controversy of definitions of the subject of the tongue. Now be sure to look at the wording! No where in the Bible are there controversies. Only in the way we translate these meanings in our own words will you find wrong. One person states that no one could tame the tongue and another declares that in order to be perfect we must control the tongue. Which one is right? Well in our church this became a real debate that ended up with hurt feelings and people leaving the church. What a shame that people can not agree to disagree. My understanding that I feel came from the Lord was that the words needed to be translated into words that can be received. The meaning of the word perfect is defined: lacking nothing essential to the whole; complete in its nature; in a state without defect. Another meaning that needs to be seen is mature or grown up. Now this definition to me is more on the line of being achievable. If I can control my tongue as a mature adult suppose to there is hope for me. On the other hand with Jesus helping me I can become mature or adult like in my speech. This would lead people to Jesus! Think about it?

It is a shame for so many people to try to be in control and so much of God's work not getting done because of the red tape that we have to go through. Our concept of organization has much to be desired and few seem to really care enough to change anything. If there was a set pattern that works for all churches it would be easier but that does not apply. Each church is different and even in the book of Revelation we can see differences that would not work in other areas. The greatest pattern to follow is the one that The Holy Spirit lays out for you. As we follow Him we will find it will link each person together in the church and give each of us a job to do. When we fail to do our job then much of the church is out of order as well. All it takes is a little problem to cause a complete melt down of the needs of the church. This is why we are given Pastors, elders, deacons, and leaders in the church. Everyone needs to get involved in an orderly fashion to bring forth much fruit.

Only too often have I heard the congregation complain about the messages from the pastor are basically the same just spoken from different angles. It seemed that no matter how I explained this no one got a hold of the way God deals with all of us. We need to understand that if we do not follow the teaching of the scripture then we do not realize what God wants from us. So the messages are continued until we get the main picture as he tries to paint it on our heart. If we start obeying the Word of God then we can move on to the next subject. Example would be prayer; all forms of prayer are emphasized most of the time because we need to be in a conversation with God continually. This is the greatest gift of our salvation and allows a presence that is victorious all the time. Yet it is a hard thing to find people that spend more that a few moments a day walking and talking in that victory. Our messages are sent from God to help us accomplish His will at the time of need. Seldom do we get the whole picture but the picture that we get should be enough to trust that He knows what He is doing and we need to obey him to become the winners.

In the most intense church we find people that truly want to serve the Lord with all they have and know. Yet the battle seems so hard that many a person has quit just before they learn enough to be victorious. We must get to the point to teach what the depth of prayer can do for anyone not just the preachers. If we can just simply teach each person to realize that when they are praying they are talking to God, then maybe we can keep them talking (praying). How can we learn the secrets of the spirit world without talking to the one in charge? There are so many deceptions coming out of the church that it is a shame. Let us get the right understanding by talking to God first and then talk to each other. Too often we are found trying to prove our own intellect that we can not learn from another. That is when we divide and find ourselves even separated from God. We are a people that need to stay together in order to be victorious. We're fighting battles that we can not see so any help we can get from another will allow us to stay in the war even longer. This should truly be the value of the church! Do you agree?

A church ministry is the greatest desire of any child of God that has been truly touched by the Lord. Many times we do not know what that is until we have learned enough about the scriptures to explain a portion of our own heart. Let us find that special place of relationship with Jesus before we worry our self sick over a ministry. Too often it is not God that is pushing us into an area that we are not comfortable in. It is often an attack to see if you will fall before you are ready to deal with all the adversity that will come with any calling. I know that in the end of time that God will do a quick work with any one that wants to serve Him, though we can be too anxious and create trouble for ourselves. Study to show ourselves approved sometimes means to learn how to deal with people, God's way. Perhaps this is a great failure in the teachings of the church or this may be one that needs to be emphasized a lot more. Either way that you can bring results that are appropriate will keep down a great deal of trouble no matter what problem may arise.

It seems that there will never be enough words to emphasize the importance of prayer on an everyday bases. Each moment we live out side the realm of heaven we need to be in touch with our Lord and Savior Jesus Christ, if for no other reason than for moral support. The help we get from Jesus can make such a difference in our way of living that even our peace of mind is affected. Most people that I have talked to over the last twenty years want all of the above at any price. Yet when it comes time to pay that price then it is always too high. We can not take that much time away from our families, job or even self to reach such a high standard. After all God knows, right? Yes I think God really knows more than we want him to. He knows that we do not want to spend that much time talking to him because of our own lust, wants, and desires that he may tell us that we should not have. Or the goals that we have set for ourselves are not his goals and we may have to change that also. Sometimes he does not approve of the way we have treated someone and we do not really want to know so we ignore him by being to busy to pray. My question is this, "does anything work when God wants to get through to you?"

One thing that I have had the joy to emphasize is that prayer changes things for the better. We seldom realize that because we tend to stop after the needs are met. When are we going to understand that prayer is conversation with God and this is our relationship with The Trinity? No one can meet your needs except Jesus and he wants a relationship built on loving conversation. How precious is that? Well unfortunately we find so many children of God that really do not talk to the Father at all. They petition, plead, or beg but never seem to get around to seeing if God wants something from them. What if our whole world was that way? Do you think God would be lonely and really feel left out from His own creation? Would you feel this way? Then why do you think we can put Him through this without it hurting our precious Father? It is my true feelings that our conversation with God makes our relationship different then just being a religion. There is more and if you will talk to him you will find out how precious he can be to us.

Most of the answers we need from our dealings with this world can be found in conversation with The Lord. So why not spend as much time as possible with Him? Much of what I have overcome from depression and from others that have gone through this pain can be attributed to The Lord. He did not cause this to come upon me yet He did see it through and allowed me to learn how to deal with it. So often the root cause was others trying to take advantage of me in one way or the other. It is a shame that people can not seem to be able to accept someone that is happier then they are. More often then not they try to steal our liberty in The Lord. When one is trying to hold us back or trying to cut off our ministry or making sure that people do not take too much creditability in what you say, then you know you are in a battle and you need to hear from The Lord. I feel like when we can not seem to get past someone that is trying to hurt us then depression easily slips in undetected but deadly. Talking with God can reveal the attack, the source and a plan to overcome to a point that it can not affect us any more. That is when you have the victory when it can not affect us. We can move on with the joy of The Lord as our strength. Amen.

There are a lot of things that can cause pain in the church and we have touched on most all of them. Yet there are still the individual events that take place every day that could keep me writing for the rest of time. Our greatest need is to be able to deal with the problems, solve them and continue to strive to go to a church that best meets our needs. A valid church first preaches the Word in its entirety and explains the blood sacrifice of Jesus so as we could have a relationship with the Father. On an individual bases, it needs to ministers to us and allows us to minister to others. When we find a church like this we also have to realize that no one wants us happy except Jesus. So the fight is on and the judgment begins. To realize this may help us stay in a church that is less than perfect. I truly believe that if we know that this is going to happen then we can fight it a lot easier and win. It is when we give up that there is no hope for the church.

Again there are many good churches that are trying to do God's will continually. We do recognize the beauty of each and know that each one is accomplishing their goals if they are following Jesus. They do not need our criticism or judgment that we put on them. They do not need our testing or ways to improve them. Most churches need to have dedicated people that love Jesus enough to put up with each other and serve Him with a sincere heart. That is the love of Jesus! Here is how to see the works of the children of God, by the love that He has given them toward the saints and the ability to overlook the many faults. When we feel like we have become spiritual then we need to examine the way we look at our brothers and sisters in the church. If we see that we can love each one of them unconditionally then we have accomplished something for Jesus and His teachings in the Bible. Here is where the rubber meets the road, are we loving or just talking? Are we praying or just saying? Are we for real or are we just trying to look good? Let us get it right and we will find Jesus!

There is so much of the time that we need boldness without being cruel. It is hard to keep one straight without entering into the other. But this is our victory when we can follow Jesus that closely. Boldness helps us to tell the truth and set the captives free according to the scriptures. We can also know Wisdom within the pages of this great book called The Bible. I would dare to say that there are answers that we have not even scratched the surface of and they are needed today. Having a streak of cruelty along with the many ways of delivering the Word of God seems way out of place. Yet daily we see the people use this method to drive home a point as they teach. Personally I feel that this method is unnecessary and find too many people have been hurt. Along with the cruelty of delivery there is also a great deal of anger that seems to always go alone with the message. The expression that comes from this is normally that this preacher is very angry at the way life has been to them. Can that be good, victorious or even helpful? Well what worked for me was not to allow this kind of delivery to enter in to steal our kindness and love. It is sad that people think we are weak by using loving kindness!

My hearts desire for many years and in every church is to reveal Jesus without compromising the message. Some times it is very hard to stay on track with all the many false teachings going on and the many people running back and forth chasing the anointing. One of the saddest things I have seen is the many people never really staying with any church long enough to become a blessing. When we are tossed about on so many winds of doctrines we often fail to get grounded and rooted. Then we are constantly destroyed by everything that can go wrong. Believe me when you can not settle in one church, it is not God's fault or anyone else's! The blame must fall entirely upon you mainly because you allow the devil to steal all you have in the Lord. Plus he takes away the many types of helps the church offers you. We are not all perfect no matter how hard we try. Though we can all be forgiven and become a blessing to the body of Christ. Instability takes away from the many manifestations of the Spirit because no one has the time to know if you are for real or not. Thus your witness never shows more than what comes out of your mouth and today that is not enough. Today one must prove the gifts by the operations and manifestations.

In the church of old many of the explanations were left out because people just simply believed in Jesus. It seems like now everything has to be proved before we can believe. This is why I fully think that the Holy Spirit does not reveal more of the manifestations. We have to see to believe and that is just opposite of what the Bible teaches. The Bible says to believe and you will see. Faith is constantly being talked about yet seldom followed except for when it involves money. This is why we have to teach on everything and explain the many doctrines of the church. Yes we should know but someday we should get it! Today we need to pray for understanding more than any other time in history. So many people are trying to get a following instead of getting people to Jesus. Or even with the best intensions people follow the anointing not the relationship we need with Jesus. Please people take your eyes off the gifts and put them on the giver of life.

The teaching of the gifts is very important to the church and has always been expressed in the realms of all churches that I know. When we seek the Giver of Life, Jesus, we find all the answers that we need. It is the job of the Holy Spirit to teach us the many differences of the offices, manifestations and the fruit of the Spirit. As we know the importance of each we need also to remember the reason is to reveal the presence of Jesus in each situation. This is the depth of the scripture as Jesus is lifted up He will draw all men unto Himself. He brings about each as there is a need where He can be glorified and honored for who Jesus is (The savior of all mankind)! The major reason for the workings in the church is salvation. Every thing else is a bonus, blessing or gift! It is hard for us to realize that the soul of man is more important than the body yet God truly does put a greater emphasize on salvation. We believe all the scriptures and pray for all to be revealed to the saints for the perfecting of the church. Yet salvation is still the greatest need! We need to pray for the manifestation of good old fashion conviction of sin more than anything else in the church today.

There is a disgusting act that comes to the heart of many a minister friend of mine that affects each of the men of God differently. That is when one supposes that they have heard a sermon before or the sermon is the same message that they personally do not want to hear. You always see it by the closing of notebooks, bible or odd looks they give their spouses or friends. Then from that point on there is this feeling that the judgment will fall and you will hear it for the next couple of weeks through every soul they talk with. There is no doubt what so ever that this does not come from God and it will benefit absolutely no one. But instead it will become their curse that will take them farther and farther away from the Lord. Most ministers I know experience this almost every sermon and can not seem to get through to the congregation the destruction that they have let their selves in for. When it is seen from the pulpit it is very hard to respond to it with love and kindness. You personally will feel the pain and aggravation that comes with the emotions of loving someone that refuses to show love under these circumstances. What is really sad is that they miss any blessing that God wishes to give them because they refuse to love back.

There is a tremendous purpose for the fruit of the Spirit as it is birthed in the heart of every new born child of God. These fruits and the maturity of them will determine how fast and constant the Lord can bless with the gifts of the Spirit. The great pain that was felt in the church of old was that of the fruit being under constant examination. It is sad to think that any one except the pastor was or will be given the gift of being a fruit inspector. I am sorry if this offends but you would be shocked at the number of children of God that have given up on the church because some one has judged them falsely and harshly. Too often we have not the Spirit of discernment to realize that the person guilty or innocent does not have the maturity to endure such pain. I do understand the need for people to understand their short comings but that can be revealed with love instead of judgment given by your interpretation of handling the situation. Love does no harm, love is kind, love is true, love is pure and love is holy unto God and man.

In the valley of decision stands most of the world as we know it today and many people are being persuaded to fall off the deep end by the example set before them in the church. No one with a heart for God wants to lead people wrong yet does so each day as they refuse to become like Jesus. Jesus said that he judged no man before his time yet if he judged it would be true. What I feel we need to understand is that until we come to the knowledge of God and decide to do things the way Jesus would, we have yet to mature enough to be judged. Because what judgment that would come could destroy our faith in God and man. Only when our faith is strong enough to endure the harsh judgment of others can we say that our faith is strong enough. Until then we are still babies and still growing up. We should always be growing in the Lord yet there should come a time where we stop hurting others just because we can. If this statement makes you mad then you have a long way to maturity in Christ, do you agree? Letting the fruit of the Spirit grow in you is one of the greatest ways you can become like Jesus. Let us work on that and see the world change before us.

Chapter Six

Our Behavior is Very Important

There is no doubt that churches fail because of man's way of running them. It could never be the will of God if the people are for real and sincere about serving and living the life that Jesus has set before them for anyone to hurt them. Churches are the people that make them up and we are not as perfect as we could be. I believe that this is something that we have to work on for our entire life. When we stop getting blessed by the messages of improving our behavior then we are on the verge of going under. There is no way to arrive in a place that we need to stop examining our way of life in word or action. If our attention is drawn away to others then we begin to judge instead of help. Yes we can look at others and not follow the examples that they set but we need to pay more attention to ourselves so as we do not fall into the same pit. When the attitudes get right and the intensions are to benefit instead of hinder then we can grow into the maturity that God desires for us. We also can stop some of the pain that is created in the church, by others and ourselves. This will obviously stop some of the splits and failures of the church.

One of the hardest things to teach in the church has also been one of the greatest reasons for the many splits and creations of great pain. The fruit of the Spirit found in the book of Gal. has always been the main source of maturity in Christ. Without eating of this fruit we can never get to the point that God can freely flow the gifts of the Spirit through us. Many people wish and pray for the gifts and yet refuse to change to be the example that is needed for the kingdom. When our life does not reflect God's love, then we tell the lost that they do not need Him. Most of the time this is where The Lord has drawn the line and stated to me that He could not use such a one like this person. Love is the very essence of our heavenly Father so how do you expect to reveal Jesus without loving unconditionally. In the church we feel that we can have the right to judge the person and refuse love when they do not stack up to our standards. The truth is that if we examine our standards no one could possibly equal such high expectations. Our witness reveals this presence of Jesus when judgment is deferred and love replaces it. As love flows so does the beauty of all the gifts to meet the needs of the ministry and the people that enter into it with us.

I believe that joy is not a tangible thing it is a heart thing. We can choose joy as we refuse to allow others to dictate to us how we wish to view this world and all the circumstances we face. Much of my life has struggled with the pain caused by others and it is hard to change that. Yet it can be changed as we allow the other fruits to prosper within. They all really do intertwine as each is needed to help the other grow and become productive to reach out to other souls. Joy is a strength that can help us keep from giving up when times dictate that there is no way we can win. When every one seems to be out to defeat the Spirit within us and either can not see, do not care how they are hurting us, this is when joy comes through. It seems when I know that I can not win and no one will allow the Spirit to move then the joy of the Lord breaks out in the laughing Spirit and I know it is going to be alright. The Lord normally allows me to be released from the burden and does not place on me any of the fear of defeat. Failure never seems to get in past the joy. This is the best way to live!

Now peace on the other hand is tangible and very much active in most people's lives. Either we have a great amount of victory through peace or we are desperately looking for just such. When there is this peace that passes all understanding that comes from the Lord then you can feel the difference in me. There is a great reward in your whole body, mind and spirit when you are at peace. Too many in the church thinks you can fake this fruit and put on a great front. But when each incident comes up the peace is gone and chaos jumps in there with the purpose of total destruction. Another give a way to the lack of peace is when the calm becomes a storm without much reason. Arguments take place on a constant bases and one can not be content unless they are the one with the solution. One always has to be right no matter how wrong they are can be another way of seeing the peace absent. Can this be an example of how hard it is to give up your will and accept God's will for your life? I truly think it is and we need to let the fruit grow in order to surrender ourselves to the Lord. It is not easy to walk with Christ Jesus but we can make it better if we only learn the simple methods to yield to the fruit of the Spirit.

Longsuffering can be a fruit that can make a difference that will allow you to minister to millions or maybe a couple in a life time. Many people want to reach the multitudes and yet a single person they can not find the ability to help. One person seems to need a lot more attention and you must be so patient and put up with the many failures. It is a hard life to serve Jesus and it takes time to be able to keep on winning instead of falling. We seem to put up with a winner but a failure we can not tolerate very long. As we grew we failed often, so why not be longsuffering with others. After all, the scripture states that God is longsuffering with us. When people see that we have this kind of fruit growing in our heart then they also feel like they can make it to the end. I truly feel that when we teach others to be so strong in their resolve then people will benefit from this teaching. Let us suffer others to hold out to the end of time and receive the reward that comes with this blessing.

The fruit of gentleness has all but been forgotten because we must be strong to survive in a world as rough as today. Sadly this is the way many children are being treated and the examples of correction in the schools are very poor indeed. Without the love of God people do not have a clue as to how to be gentle, firm and consistent with all the people they deal with daily. Gentleness is by no means weakness as some try to teach. When power is needed God provides the proper ability to handle anything. Yet there is this consistent loving gentleness that overflows the heart that can be felt by all. When we sell out to Jesus this fruit can make a difference in any family and ministers to the world with a victory that few can actually explain. Though we truly know it is for real.

How does one explain goodness? We make the statement of being good constantly yet the expression sometimes gets lost with the desires of our heart. This part of the fruit is a state of being that can give one great freedom from any type of oppressing spirit. The reality of our actions that overcome any evil with humble expressions of good words, works or behavior refuses to allow any attachments of spirits that do not belong to God. There for sickness, disease or pain does not belong and can not stay. In always providing ourselves with this type of protection we set the type of example that is different then the world and people want to be a part of the blessing. Not everyone will be desirous to pay or pray the price for this type of behavior but it is available to all those who are walking right with God. In the state of being good we must also keep in mind not to flaunt such as a superior being or something. Keep yourself humble and see the great affect that God can have on others with this fruit alive in your heart.

Now faith is a subject that has had millions of books wrote about and can not be exhausted. Too many try to express every idea that crosses their mind to teach how to receive and activate faith. Yet to me faith is an action more than a thing. We must keep on serving Jesus with an open mind and an ear to hear what He has to say to all mankind. I do not have to activate faith or exercise it. All I have to do is seek the face of Jesus and His righteousness and He will allow enough faith to believe for anything. The time spent in seeking Jesus will determine the amount of faith I have on any subject. Also the success that I have had trusting God adds to the measure of faith. What we see really does allow us to trust Him more. As we reach for a greater way of glorifying Jesus we can find a greater outreach into the gifts of the Spirit. Remember to always be searching for ways to bring glory and honor to the Lord and you could have the favor needed to receive the anointing to get the job done. It is the anointing that breaks the yoke.

Now the last of the fruit of the Holy Spirit is temperance and there is good reason for it to be last. Beyond a shadow of a doubt it is the hardest fruit to develop. When we can get a hold of the fact that without self control there is little hope for the blessings of God, then we will find ourselves seeking The Lord like never before. It is not only hard to control our temper but every aspect of our life needs to come under the subjection of The Holy Spirit. Time and discipline are just as important to get the jobs that we are given done. This part of self control is hardly talked about and we seldom try to realize its importance. As we try to control the environment around us, we find it is nearly impossible. Every time I want to study the Word of God there are hindrances that constantly come up. In the work of the Holy Spirit there is this discipline that I can call on and put off every trick of the evil one and study. Another way of control is getting up early before all the rat race begins to interfere with my prayer life. This is extremely important because it helps us to start the day with the Lord and allow Him to begin to lead our daily life into victory. We can truly live from glory to glory instead of from defeat to defeat. Think about it? Temperance is a very hard fruit to grow yet it is so rewarding that you can not leave it out.

I find it very strange that so many churches feel that they can build a church by the gifts of healings and miracles. I have not seen one really effective. Too often we get our eyes off of the one creating the gifts and loose sight of the needs of the ministry all together. When we loose sight of Jesus and His desire to save the lost and reach the outcast than we have missed a lot. The gifts are to follow the Word not replace it. Too often the people want to see the miracles and not want to hear how to change their own lives to be like Jesus. Thus many are following a man/woman instead of seeking out Jesus for themselves. The way you can tell is when a person falls these followers of man/woman are devastated defeated and leave the church. Many never enter church again. Normally there will be all kinds of excuses but no real reason. We need to pray for the pain in the churches for all those that want to follow a person instead of Jesus and build the church on Him and not mankind.

We are told to allow the Holy Spirit to use us to manifest the fruit and gifts of the Lord. In so doing we can reveal the Lord Jesus and all His great love. How can we see the blessings of the Lord if we do not let Him work through us? Why would we ever think that any of Jesus' works could be in our own strength? The good news is all about Jesus and His saving grace! No other direction should ever catch our attention even for a moment. As we focus upon Jesus we can rest assured that our trust will never be in vain. The blessings are for all God's children and we need the relationship to be real, close and powerful. That is when the miracles become constant and continual. That is when it becomes easy to share Jesus with the lost and all His great power. This is truly when the life we live is very exciting, blessed and precious in the sight of every one we meet. This is when people realize that our life is different than the world around us and they want to be a part of just that.

It seems like the more we try to be like Jesus the more the battle increases and the greater our need is for the depth of His love. When we feel like we have arrived it is time to break out the big guns and fast and pray earnestly. Though we can move on from glory to glory it is still just a drop in the bucket in comparison to the depth of God's greatness. The more I learn about Him the more I realize that there is much to learn. There have been unbelievable changes in my life and every day that I am true to myself and Jesus I find there is a lot of improvement needed. When I feel there is no judgment left in me then something comes up and The Lord reveals to me the way I am looking at the problem is wrong. As

I feel that I can minister to anyone then someone shows up that turns me completely sour. In repentance and tears there is still little I can do for one that has already felt the inner emotions that I could not hide. Though we feel like a conquering hero then we are devastated by something we thought could never happen, at least to us. The more I see of life the greater the need for Jesus to take my hand and lead me safely on down the path He has for me. So my love and need for Him grows more each moment of every day. Are we so different?

In order to understand the different needs of the church we must first understand the difference in people and we have to see the ability to love them where they are. That is really hard to see when we want them to grow up at a rate that is equal to where we are after being in the ministry twenty years or so. It is the shame of all the church that we can not distinguish the maturity of an individual and treat them accordingly. Not to baby them to death or to push them off the deep end but to love them into a place they can receive from God in order for them to grow according to the ability that God have given them. Though this should not have to be said, we need to have the patience to deal with them through the eyes of Jesus (without judgment). If we saw people with God's eyes then we would have the love, compassion and concern to bring them along with us into maturity and the fullness of Christ. Then we could see the fruit grow before we expected the gifts to be working. We could see the changes being made in their personality no matter how slight that might be. Oh, how much healthier a person would be developed mentally, physically and spiritually right in front of our eyes. Do you think that would make us proud? Here is even a better question, how much do you think Jesus would be proud of them and us?

So much of the pain in the church has been from very impatient people that have no time for anyone but their family. In reverse the pastor is accused of spending too little time with their own family. There needs to be a balance between the two. Most pastors feel closer to their church family and there for that is where they are needed. Where the family states, do not preach at me, the church wants to know what God has to say. How much easier is it to be who God has made you instead of dividing yourself up into the husband, father, grandpa, and friend to each person? It is easy to say that everyone understands that we are the head of the family but it is the dividing yourself that does the separating in our own minds. I have not met a pastor that does not struggle with this or a church member that understands. Most families come to a point that they just say that this is the way it is going to be. If the patience is so slack with the pastor, is it no wander that there is so little patience with a new child of God? This is where we all need to work, fast and pray to help each other do the many things that God has asked us to in the church. This kind of growth leads to maturity. Let us work at it!

Families are seldom more demanding than anyone can handle. Yet the church can expect so much from the pastor that he has no family life what so ever. Many a leader in the church demands just this type of service from the man of God and as a way to achieve this he has to give up everything to be there. The scripture used the most is when Jesus was talking to his disciples and told them if they can not give up everything for Him they are not worthy of Him. Well this is true there is no contradiction in the bible. If you have the ability to search out the heart of the pastors that truly give their service to the Lord Jesus you will find that they have given up everything in their life to follow Him. When there is a choice the family always takes the back seat and normally has no problem with that. Yet there are the times that God sets aside for the man of God to rest, study, reach out and spend time with the family in order for all things to be fulfilled in their lives. What joy can a family have when they have no time together? How can we live a full life if it is only in the church and the home is incomplete? Dear children, if the home is not secure, neither will the church have the type of stability it needs!

Love is the victory of all fruit, power and joy of our salvation both public and private. Where we have trouble in the area of love we also have trouble in receiving from God. Since God is love we must come to the point of loving even the unlovable. Too often we miss out on this great blessing due to race, looks or temperament. Here is where the break threw must take place to allow us to find the truth to be free from the disobedience of not loving. Here is the key that I have found when I have trouble loving someone. In the place of the person or persons I list Jesus in my mind and love Him for them. Sometimes that is real hard when they have hurt you but it is always the right thing to do and the greatest victories come from that process. You see as long as you can not love a person they can control your emotions every time you see them or when they come across your thoughts. I have found it very draining when others control or try to control me. In the church people use the expression of divine inspiration. To me it is manipulation which denies love and needs to be avoided. So I love Jesus in their place!

Time is one of the few things in the world that we can manipulate. Either we use it wisely or we waste what chances we have to accomplish the task God has for us. We have noticed that there are few times that we can find a new friend and make this a lasting relationship in Christ. Each time we have passed it over for what ever reason there has not been another time that we can be there for them. Sad but true. It is time to reach out like never before to take hold of every chance to make friends in the church universal. As well as learning the different ways to reach lost souls even if it does not work for you. The attempt will make a difference and never come back void. Try always to keep your eyes open to find the people that God puts in your path to reach for His Name sake. We as the entire body of Christ, need each other like never before and can draw from the strength that is provided. We can not accept just anything as a form of religion and join them. We must hold tight to the truth of our faith in Jesus' atonement for sin. For there is no other Name that man can be saved but in the name of Jesus Christ the only begotten of the Father. So use your time wisely, make friends and reach out for lost souls.

Some of our greatest failures come from the different type of worry in the church that goes to the point of torment. Too often we bank all our cards on the events that we set up to draw the crowds and if they do not work the fear/worry sets in. Did we do the right thing? Was God in it? Was we anointed enough? Did we pray enough? Did every one do their job right? Was there enough cooperation? Were we one in the Spirit? Oh, do you see the turmoil that takes place when more than likely the event was a huge success? Then on top of that there is this lack of responsibility that most in the church seem to stay in. They begin to accuse when they feel like it could have been better if it had gone their way. What a mess we are even though we think we are on top of the world? Is it no wander that most pastors declare that we are only a church by the grace of God? Truly I see now more than I ever did when I was a pastor and I pray that my understanding has increased tremendously. I feel that the Lord should allow each pastor to stand back at a distance to reflect upon the church and see what is going on and what needs to happen. Maybe then we can eliminate some of the pain and much of the horrible effects of church splits.

The feelings of the old ways have always been a theme in most every church that I have had the joy to visit. Yet when people start talking about the old ways, they do not realize that they are not always accurate. The old ways were bent on soul winning as number one, healing as number two and deliverance as number three. Everything else was extra or things they wanted to do. The crowds came to hear the Word and see people get saved, delivered and set free from sin. Healings and miracles were the following results of obedient servants with much prayer and fasting. Back then if you wanted to move God you fasted. If you wanted to see your loved ones saved, you fasted. If you wanted to see healings, you fasted. If you wanted to see people delivered from demon activity, you fasted. If you wanted to see a miracle, you guessed it, you fasted. You see when the children of old were taught that they needed to bring their body under subjection to God, they just simply did it. Because that has and will always move Him with compassion and we will see results. What we are missing in most people's lives are results of the movement of God. When results are missing, empty or hollow or do not last people do not find anything to follow. Thus they do not truly see the reason for God to be in their life. That is why we need to learn from the old ways.

In the church of today you hear all these demands, orders given and barked out authority to shake the very heart of men and women. From what I see is that this is simply to get people to obey the Word of God. What ever happened to the contrite and humble spirit of leaders? Have we become so cold to The Spirit of God that we can not hear His heart? So we have to force people into submission or make them obey. Folks this should not be the norm in the church! Along with the anointing of God comes the wisdom to gain the confidence of the people. We need to apply this wisdom in dealing with the saved and lost in order to fulfill the work of the church in a pleasing way. When those of a contrary spirit are put in charge or given authority, we find a struggle that should not be. As people wish the power instead of the will of God we also see such a battle. When one wishes to use their authority for their advantage we see great destruction. Yesterday was no different, we just did not hear of it as often because it was an internal matter. Today with every thing in the spot light we see all this trying to represent the church, we should understand why it is so hard to get people to come and be a part.

The surrendering of the past pain of the church is very hard to come by due to the constant reminders from everyone that knew any thing about the church of old. There is entirely too little forgiveness in the church and sad enough to say it has always been this way. We learn that if we forgive that the Father will forgive us for Jesus' sake. Yet we continue the pain of constantly hurting some one else. The way you know this is every time you see someone getting attention in the church the rumors are started up again. That turns people away from them and the attention is stopped. Sadly enough so is the will of God. What God has put on my heart to say is this action is WILLFUL SIN. There must be a time that this action stops or some wrapped up in this sin will not make heaven! My heart does not cry out for vengeance, it cries for the truth to be revealed so as one would repent and get right with God. Our Father is a loving God and He does not want anyone to suffer through this, it is time to put the past to rest, forgive and get on with the work that God wants every one to do.

There is a banner that every one should be striving to receive from the precious Father of lights. This banner is not hard to achieve but it is vital to the church, self and all around each Christian. That is the banner of love! Throughout this book this has been expressed many ways and yet here is another way that God wants it to be brought out. The greatest weapon of our warfare is that of Love as God ordains. Many a child of God expresses this fact yet fails to live in its security. Love maintains a balance of all the fruit, gifts and manifestations of the Holy Spirit. The way of it does come from the old saying that love does no harm to anyone. Our lives must reveal this attribute in order to allow God to show how precious a gift Jesus really was and can be. When love rules freely and openly there are people that can be reached no matter how hard they are. With the peace of God showing the benefits of this great love people can see another life style that is impossible to beat. If we get this we will become soul winners for Jesus. As He put it, fishers of men.

So often I have seen the trials of the oppressed and tormented from the things of the world that people think they can not do with out. Too much of the worldly things have crept into the church that we look the same in our entertainment, praise and worship. We take on all the attributes and wonder why the people are not breaking down our church doors to get in. I believe that we need to ask ourselves, why do we go to church? What is the purpose and meaning of the church? Are we to be different than the world? One of our past failures was the fact that we wanted to be entertained more than we wanted to hear the Word and change to the likeness of God. We are to love unconditionally, treat people like ourselves, care for those who have no one and help others to help themselves. Build up the fallen, support The needy, aid the wounded and reveal how Jesus can make a difference. Our mission should be all about Jesus and reaching lost souls and not ourselves. We need to define the purpose for the church. We truly need to know what we are doing in order to stop the pain that takes the focus off Jesus. Do you agree?

When the eyes of the church are open they often find suffering all around them that they have never seen before. It is a shame that suffering is all around us but we become insensitive to it. The blood and guts of television has all but taken away all the moral standards that used to thrive in the church. This also influenced the entire community yet today we find little knowledge of the existence of the church. We need to be making a difference in our community and drawing attention to the sinful decisions made. Most people want to be on a crusade of some nature, so why not start one for God and what is right in the world. Why not expose sin for what it is, death? Separation from God! The denial of The Holy Scripture and the failure to stand up for all that Jesus died for on the cross. This is what we are surrendering to the world one step at a time. I know that the scripture prophecies this in the last days and I say folks we are in the last days. Church open your eyes we are being invaded by the world government and the hate crime laws that are intended to help the suffering. Yet these are being manipulated to attack the church. It may be covertly but it is still happening, let us not only pray it through let us fight for our rights in the church.

Do you think that some of the demon possession is isolated to the past or just for the very young? With the battles that are taking place to conquer all the Houses of God we need to see the attack we are under. Never before have we been under such an attack of confusion where the Word of God becomes so twisted. We have many books that are very good and help others to find the meanings of the scripture. Yet never should we replace the scripture with any other book. No matter how good it is or what affect it may have The Bible is still God's Word to the people. There is no controversy, fear or doubt so go by the Word of God! There may be a misunderstanding in the way others think and express themselves. A million other problems could have been placed in their book. God has blessed many a child of God to express his will in the understanding of what is going on in the world today and I feel that there has been some great books that helped me a lot. Yet the Bible is my source to find our Savoir Jesus and His answers for my life. His hope and promises are true and His Word will never pass away or loose its power to change lives. So remember to not open yourself up to controversy or the tricks of the devil to overcome the scripture. Hold on to the truth in the Word of God and He will never fail you.

We must understand that people sometimes get tired of doing what is right. There are weak points in our walk with God that we listen to the devil and fall into this type of trap. In these moments there are real temptations to do something wrong. Normally the major sins we can avoid, it is the little problems that we fall into. Lies, rumors, gossip or judgment of others are some of the ways we can do such hurt and feel like its okay. You know the conviction falls yet you continue until The

Lord has to get your attention. Why do we have to get to that state? Can we stay close enough to Jesus to avoid such times of weakness? I think we can if we just realize how much it bothers The Holy Spirit every time we take our attention away from Him. The Spirit is gentle and loving and it does not take much to hurt Him. We do not have to live in fear yet we should live in love with God enough to be sensitive to the Holy Spirit. He is the one that reveals the will of God, The Father and Jesus our savior. He shows us how to act like Jesus and be one that God would be proud of. It is not always so easy to do the right thing but it is the best way to show God our love for him. Living that way also gives us our best witness. So let us do our best and endure the temptations by doing right. Then we will surely find the life of blessings that God has for us.

Our path is often clouded over or hazed to the point that hard decisions are difficult. We look for the will of God and often when we discuss this with some one else in the church our answers are normally no. We are not good enough. Well, maybe no one tells you that but they show that with their criticism and pathetic facial expressions. So often I have even seen a minister look to just certain people to draw strength from because others would bring them down. People we need to find the potential in every body in the church no less the children. Even the least in the church could be doing more good than the highly recognized. If we could only see their prayer life we could surely know more about them. Our prayer worriers are enabling each of us to reach the lost and help others to grow (mature) in the ways of God.

Are they less important then the minister? I think not! Without them the church does not move at all. Should we realize that that person being criticized may actually reach more people than any one else in the church and they need my prayers, wisdom and teaching to become what God wants them to be? For me it is easy to see my children become the greatest spiritual leaders in the world but how about that one that has no one in their corner?

There are many open doors in this world and our Father will see to it that your door of ministry will open at just the right time. When I think of all the mixed up children of the world it troubles me to see the different messages coming out of the pulpits today. We are not all unified and it is hard to choose what the true doctrines are. Most people that are raised in a particular church can stand on that doctrine. Yet there are many people that have not had that experience so it is very difficult for them. We must be cheer leaders for them and directors to the one and true Jesus. This way He can lead them in the direction they need to go. Most of the time it is a family member or relative that gets one to go to their church and that is great. One thing that we need to see is that when we lead some one to church and do not stay with a certain church, we leave a very confusing message. When all we find is fault in a church there will never be the right one for that person. Normally it is just a short time that our followers are driven away from churches all together. What is really sad is when I hear the statement that they do not understand why they are out of church.

Folks when you are not stable or can not stay in a church to help it become stable, the people you are trying to lead could not be. God help us to become stable in our homes, jobs and churches. Lord Jesus, help us follow you.

What I have found in my personal life was the need to have a daily devotional and lots of prayer. On the devotional we see the constant reaching for a deeper walk with God and what better way can we receive that then studying His Word? When The Word is taken in content we can find the deeper meanings that will apply to our lives today. Yes we need to see the settings of yesterday and allow for the reflection of today to bring understanding. As we do so the Word will come alive and bless beyond measure. The very first need we have is to pray and ask the Holy Father to explain the benefit of our daily journey in the scripture. Then too do not let it become boring. Put yourself into the characters that you are reading about and let it be meaningful to you. What if I were John the Baptist at the river when Jesus came by and I saw the Spirit ascend upon Him? What type of an impact would that have on me? Would my eyes be opened to His glory or would I miss the importance of the event? You see this is just one example of a million that could benefit you greatly. If you are going through the scripture talking to The Lord there could be such a bonus that it can change your life for ever. If you have no time for the scripture and prayer you can expect that your changes and blessings will come very slow.

The old adage of if you do not believe in something you will fall for anything is very true. In the church we have given in to the concept of acceptance that we fail to give the true example of Christ. Any more it is not what would Jesus do, it is would Jesus say that! Would He use vulgarity, would He speak words to offend, would He set out to degrade people, would He abuse with words? Think this out and spend some time in prayer and fasting. If any of these answers come to you as a yes than you did not hear from God! If you set out to break down a persons potential to succeed than you have said something that Jesus would not say. Some times we break the will of God without meaning to by just simply not letting a person grow to the point of success. Constantly disapproving of them and battering them with words that tear down or hurt feelings. This normally brings anger and quenches the proper results that God is trying to get from that one. Many times the immature will just simply quit. What is so wrong about this is that we are directly responsible even if we do not agree. The failure of those around us can very well be ours. Think about it!

Have you ever asked yourself this question, "Would Jesus think like that or would He have these thoughts? You see I believe that if we would consider these questions before we respond to anything that someone could throw at us, we would act totally different. Would Jesus think of evil thoughts or speak evil words at us? Would Jesus set out to destroy our witness? Would He ruin our ministry? Would He attempt to break our spirit or reputation with rejection or bitter rumors? How would Jesus respond to your vulgar or suggestive words? What about off colored jokes? What about your ethnic nick names or put downs? Where would we think that Jesus would approve of the constant put downs of other ministries when we are trying to prove them wrong, especially, if we lie about what they believe. You see even if we do not know and declare something, I believe that is a lie. What would Jesus do is very powerful but what would he think or say is also just as powerful.

In my attempts of finding the reasons that people hurt others and call it acceptable in the eyes of God, I have not really found. All I have found is personal sin. Sadly enough most of this pain has been willful and belligerent acts. Whether it is for revenge or any type of personal satisfaction the hurt has been devastation. One in particular action I witnessed was when a person in the church was trying to hide sin in their life. When this was revealed this person did not turn to Jesus, as was the intent but turned to attack me with lies and rumors. Sad enough to say is that this has gone on for nearly twenty years. All the time I was a pastor the attack continued. When I surrendered the church to another pastor, then every where I visited this person would go to the pastor and spread the same lies. After the pastors saw the anointing on my life they wrote off the lies and rumors and wanted me to stay and minister with them. One reason or the other God has moved me around to help different churches and the same mess would creep up like a serpent in the woods. There were several years that I would confront this person in all the scriptural ways to no avail. Then God told me to turn them over to Satan and I did. Though it constantly comes up and a few pastors have joined in on trying to defame me, God has been faithful with His love, anointing and blessings on my family. When God approves your ministry, who is man?

Today the power of God and His precious Son, Jesus is still alive in my heart to reach out to others that have experienced the same or similar hurts. If we could just learn to keep our eyes off of others I believe we could live a much happier life and all those around us would be better off also. Man and woman alike have a hard enough time living the life that God has set before them without our hindrance. How often did Jesus up braid the religious people for turning their traditions to become more important then the Word of God? What makes us think that we are free from the judgment that we place upon others? There are way too many tears being shed each time the children come together in judgment of others. A dear child of eighteen made a mistake and sinned against God through fornication. Odd enough only once was enough to bring forth a child into the world. The elders of the church passed judgment, (after she repented and asked the church to forgive her of the sin) that she with the child was to be removed from the church because it was a constant reminder of her sin. The explanation given was that if she had of aborted the child they could have forgiven her. Yet this child was a disgrace to the church. I never knew that murder was a lesser crime then fornication. God help us realize all the lives we destroy because of the lack of wisdom and the knowledge of God's Word.

There is a two fold problem in the church today that has always been around. One is having too much time to work on evil thoughts or ways to get attention. The other is too little time to reflect upon God's Word for understanding. The first I have addressed in great detail let us talk about too little time. My heart breaks every time some one tells me that there is no way they are going back to church again to be hurt so bad. No one is going to get another shot at me! When people have too little time to talk with God they have this feeling that they need to talk about others or look into their life. It is so sad to think that we can ever see all of any one's heart since it is hidden from every one except God. Normally we will find that even after living with someone for twenty years or so that there are many things we have never known. How can we possibly think that we can know someone that we may see three times a week for a couple hours and then do not talk to them? How is it that we can listen to what others say about someone and think we know them well enough to figure them out? It is not hard for any one to realize that Satan has crept into the church to do damage and most of the time it is undetected. The motives and intentions of a heart can only be read by our Lord Jesus so why not go to the one who knows? Why not ask, is this of you Lord? Did you tell them to do this? Can you see, too little time with God?

In searching out the motives and intentions of one's heart we must understand that there are many factors that may never come to light. Most true Christians do not want to hurt anyone so they set out to avoid these things that they know will hurt. This is where we often miss the mark in our understanding. Our hearts should be working close to God to get through the pain and not cause any further hurt. Here is why we work on many projects to reveal correction without embarrassment or pain. In our sermons and Sunday school teachings we find the Lord trying to open us up to the pain we have created for others. Only when we recognize the revelation do we attempt to correct ourselves or when we are exposed to everyone. Over and over again I have heard that someone would say that the preacher had been talking to someone about what they did. That answer is normally true, they had been talking to God and he wanted to straighten out the problem. Our failure to correct ourselves, often open us up to punishment or to the traps of the devil that makes it even worse.

Chapter Seven

Victory With Jesus in the Church

On reflection of the past church and the church of today there are some definite realities that play a part in the pain of others. These realities must be looked at from the individual view point of the one that was hurt. There are today millions of books wrote to help us with building or adding to the church. Though there are not many wrote to help us deal with the hurt the church has created. Please remember as we deal with the hurt the church is the people that attend that assembly. Therefore we are dealing with the people who belong. Most every one in the church belongs that are right with God and those who do not belong can by getting right. Salvation is the common denominator between anyone.

When pain comes from the lost it is easier to recognize and overcome. When our family (the church) hurts us it is a pain that can take years to get over. That is why I believe that the sermons are intended to head off the pain before it can take root and destroy. We need to recognize our every action toward others, seize the opportunity to make amends, be quick to forgive and ask for forgiveness, and to act in such a way as to please The Holy Spirit that lives within our heart. Any quenching or holding back from the unction of The Spirit normally will cause pain.

Here is something that I feel is of the utmost importance to all Christians and we must teach our new children the same. God's love is perfected in us as we love our brother and sister in Christ. How can you love your brother and sister in Christ if you will not even go to church with them? Where is your victory in the combined power of the saints if it is not in church? When can we expect a movement of God if He mainly moves in the church? Are we going to share God's greatest blessing with the church? How about the gifts that He plants within us? What about the anointing that breaks the yokes? I know that the pain in the church makes us want to give up on all churches everywhere. Yet children, we are greatly needed in the body of the church to help change the many people that want to cause pain. If they only see others that want the pain then they will never find a way out of the world's way of thinking. How can you make a difference if you are always running from the problems? Is it possible to bring light into the church to expose the sin if you are not there to teach the truth? Your voice can be heard even when no one wants to change. You do make a difference if you do not run before God is done with you in any situation or church. Every excuse will fall idol and void when we stand before God and try to explain away our failure to make a difference. I pray with all my heart that you will be able to say that you stood your ground in the churches to reveal the truth of God's Word and loved as He gave us commandment.

Throughout the history of the church it has been apparent that the greatest people God has identified are the ones that had a solid relationship with Jesus. The friends of God have always been the most successful in life. We see this as we receive him as Savior and begin our walk. Yet as we learn more of the Word of God we almost replace the relationship with the knowledge of the Word. Some even go as far as declaring they are the same. There is something very special in realizing that a personal talk with Jesus is better than all the knowledge we can gain. Knowing about Jesus and knowing Him has got to be distinguished. Our desire to know the Word is balanced by the presence of The Holy Spirit that reveals Jesus and His fullness. That can only come from the conversations with our Lord and Savior Jesus. Hear is where the heart is complete and a friend we can become as we make the relationship personal. Hold on to all the knowledge that The Word can teach you and hold on to the loving hand of Jesus as you walk through this life. Between the wonderful grace of The Father and the wisdom of the Word of God we can find our way through this life victorious. We can also find that very little can happen to us that the relationship with our most faithful friend can handle.

As I walk deeper in the Lord I find that the relationship means more than anything and only through that relationship will we find the overcoming power to defeat the enemy of our soul. Actions speaks louder than words, was only a clique at one time, now it is fact. Reasoning with all the words in the Bible would not convince someone about faith in God if they do not want to believe. There seems to be a lack of words when it comes to those that would not accept faith as a jumping off point into the presence of God. It is hard to believe when the mind is closed to anything except facts so where do we go? The truth of the matter is that debate, argument or discussion will seldom break down the door. But prayer in faith believing will bring The Holy Spirit on the seen to reveal Jesus and the truth about God the Father. Unless they can believe that He exist it will be very hard to see them find the reward. You see hope is not what you see but what you believe and faith in Jesus is everything. We sometimes forget that when one is not saved they do not even consider a conversation with God. To them that is way out of their reach. It takes the Holy Spirit in their heart to convince them otherwise. We need to believe that The Holy Spirit will continue to draw them to faith in the living God.

Borrowed images and ideas would not get through to The Lord as some people think. When it comes to all religions are correct and there are many ways to get to God, well that is a borrowed idea. The barrowed image is that we can find God in everything. Everything does exist because of Him and all sins can be forgiven through the blood shed on Calvary by Jesus Christ the righteous but God is not in everything. There is nothing that can contain God for He declares that He is Spirit. Not like water that can be held in a glass or a physical body that is confined to the gravity of the earth. Jesus in the resurrected form is body and spirit, was not bound by anything either. All man, all God, not held by time and space but ever living in the supernatural form. Now I can not explain any deeper than that but I believe the facts of the Holy Scripture by the evidence place in my heart through faith in Jesus. To me this is the difference in all religions we have a Savior that died for our sins and came back to life to live with us through the Holy Ghost that is alive in our hearts. He is our hope and seal of Salvation that gives us a working relationship with the Father God. So by faith do not hinder the Holy Spirit, do not shut Him out, do not quench His call to salvation but yield to Him and believe that Jesus died for us and God raised Him from the dead to pay for our sins. Then ask Him to come inside our hearts to live with us and show us how to live pleasing to God.

All things are sold by beauty, popularity or what seems to be good for us. Instead of the old fashion belief in God and the understanding that beauty is only skin deep and popularity can lead you astray. Every thing sold today either appeals to the sexual apatite or the idea that this will make you popular, up to date or more noticed. If the average church goes by this we can look around the room and find out that the jobs will soon run out of people to do them. Our way of looking at people is totally different then God's. It is time we got back to the anointing of The Holy Spirit to determine who will fulfill God's will. The Lord told me once to look for the people who were doing the job on their own and give them the position and authority to get it done. When we support these people then God can bless the church as well as trust us with the many gifts. A person needs to be tried as well as held accountable this alone will keep them trying to serve God right. Let us open our eyes and see who it is that is working and blessing.

In the many circles of the church we need to look at the circle of leaders and their responsibility to God. The past has opened up a door of approval through achievement. What have you gotten done, no matter how you have hurt people to get there? This to me is totally unacceptable! We need high achievers but not at the expense of the children of God. The greatest need is to allow the fruit to grow in everyone so we all keep from hurting each other. We do not have to kill someone to get anything done or even ourselves. Our faith should keep us on the right track to accomplish the goals that God set before us without all the pressure that we impose upon everyone around us. Can we get it done without falling apart? You see it is when we feel overwhelmed that I believe the pressure becomes a torment and torment is not of God. We need good organization without harsh dictation. Too often our past has shown us that to be heard we must command with force. In the church this way of doing anything only causes pain, doubt and confusion as the standard set before us. The question that comes is how can we be this way and be of God? Someday we will find out exactly how many times we failed to accomplish anything because of this type of leadership. As for me, I do not want to be a part of this crowd that will cause me to hang down my head before God and realize the failures. What about you?

In eliminating some of the pain created in the church we must consider the conversation of our heart. As we stand strong in faith we can only show the right example when we speak in such a way that our faith can see results. Our conversation must be positive and built upon the Word of God. When we speak in doubt, half hearted or not very sure of the results it often hurts the listeners' faith. This always hinders Gods response to the prayer and the child you are praying over either does not come back or feels like they are not worthy to receive God's best. Unanswered prayers are not always a result of sin many times they are the result of a lack of understanding of the Word of God and knowledge of what He wants for you. Before we pray for anything we should go to The Lord with praise and worship seeking the will of God for the subject. After that we can pray with confidence that The Holy Spirit will lead the prayer in the right direction for the best results. Of course this means to do the hardest act that we can find, waiting upon the Lord for His answer. Too often we brush past The Holy Ghost thinking He will respond to us, instead of us responding to Him. When we respond to Him we pray right and see the best results even when the answers are, no. Consider your conversation as you pray for others and expect to see the results by faith.

In our search for ending the pain in the church we must consider that we may not end all of it. Yet we can do much better as the subject is not swept under the rug and ignored. Too often we allow these battles to take place and think that it will go away if we do not confront them. Unfortunately Satan is too wise for that because when he sees us being passive he attacks with all the power he can to destroy lives. The very popular pastors are noncombatant and many times a problem will explode before it can be stopped or healed. When that happens the problems are seldom solved without tremendous pain involved. Therefore it may take years before there will be a reconciliation. It is better to treat people right all the time and avoid all of this. But since we will not, we need to always be ready to minister to broken relationships with others and with God. Let us search out God's answers and minister with an open heart full of love. Expect to see the miracles of our Lord and Savoir Jesus for He is the only one that can read the heart clear enough to make a difference in our lives. Love is the key, Jesus is the way!

Reconciliation can become a battlefield within itself and can take years before we see the results that God wants. We all seem to want to live in peace and yet when it comes to admit our part of the wrong, well, we just do not. The true power of being humble comes into play as The Holy Spirit gives us the ability to admit the truth and do something about it. More times than not I have had to accept the blame because people are not close enough to God to want to make amends. Why someone would rather live in pain, heartache or emptiness of a broken friendship, I do not know? It is easy to change if we allow The Holy Spirit to have reign in our hearts. I truly feel that it is easier to give up the hurt then to give up on a friendship that has been a benefit to me. Friends are usually there for you even though you are wrong. They tell you the truth and pray until you see it and make things right. If they do not stay with you in the bad times, they are not your true friend in the first place.

Year after year I have searched the world and all the body of Christ in our community and have found maybe three friends. Sad to say that once you enter into the pain of church problems no one cares enough for you to be there. The excuse I have heard the most is that if I associate with them I am condoning their actions. Therefore I am following the scripture in turning them over to Satan to buffet them with the hope of them returning to the right path. Most of the time the pain is so severe that without support one may never return, no less if one is innocent. God for bid if the church is ever accused of hanging an innocent person! I am not trying to hang fault on anyone or even blame. It is enough to realize that the problems exist in a huge way and many are the souls that suffer from such abuse. We can really help people in these circumstances and keep or bring them back into the church. But there needs to be a change of mind when it comes to the way we look at all problems in the church. We must see people as they really are, guilty yet forgiven. They are washed in the blood of Jesus and just as good as any of the rest of us. People need to know that their gifts are needed in the church and we need to accept and train them. God help us all to be friends just as Jesus is our friend.

Our days on earth are very limited and really seem insignificant in comparison to eternity. Yet we as children of the Most High God have this obligation that He would not let us renege on. Even though we are not to be a part of this world's evil actions we must remain here working to lead people to Jesus. When our name is called in Glory we shall be out of here but until then let us try to work together without pain. It is enough to be hurt by the church people you love but it is even worse to be the one that causes the pain. All throughout our lives God has given us the time to make a difference in other's lives. Let us not blow it by stupid things like ego, self-recognition or the desire to be a leader. People think that we have to have people to be the rod of correction in and out of the church. I think that is an excuse to hurt people and is not necessary at all. Jesus is the head of the church and can handle every problem with the means that do not destroy lives. One of our desires that hurt so much is the need to make an example of anyone. This could not come from God because every time I have seen this applied in the church it has failed in bringing someone back to Jesus. Instead it has hurt many lives that was not originally apart of the problem. Do you ever think we will learn?

Do you think that you will ever teach people to line up with us so as they will be a part of the movement of God? Well, I have heard this statement a lot in the last twenty years and have noticed the many flaws spoken. First of all our judgment of others and their participation is always off. We never seem to give credit to the ones that pray any movement of God into existence. No less the one God uses to expose the need or the way to bring out the process to get it done. One of the examples of this is: I have always had the desire to help people yet seldom know how. The Lord always seems to let some one else tell me of the need. Someone that brings the need to light deserves just as much credit as I do. Another thing we need to recognize is that seldom if ever the movement of God is just for one person or even one part of the Body of Christ. God touches every one around you when He touches you! Believe me when I say that God has no problem in ministering to the many as He ministers to one. Let us remember that God's plans are multi-purposed. There are many things that can be accomplished in any movement. We need to be in one accord but not always lining up to one person. Or else how could we reach the different task if we are only looking to one's interpretation. I truly believe that our greatest failure is that only one person hears from God. We only need one leader but when there are many things to get done we need every one's input.

Opening the door to accomplish any task we must understand that if we use many different people we must use great wisdom to include everyone. The hardest thing is to know each one's potential and what are their best gifts. Placing each one is not so hard unless one does not know their place and gift. When one is a giver and they want to prophecy instead they throw off the whole plan of unified work. As one barks out commands instead of humbly giving their selves to the labor they cause hurt feelings continually. If we would simply realize the greatness of humility we could be apart of any group and accomplish task that otherwise would never happen. Let us open up to The Holy Spirit and learn how important each person really is and find peace in lifting up the other person. Then maybe we can truly be a blessing to most any church we go into. My experience is that people find this place of favor with the work they are doing and would not give that up.

After a while we may get stale and could use a replacement, even if it only last for a short time. Any help to get refreshed will always be a great blessing. When that kind of help comes it should always be recognized.

Here is another place of pain we should address. In our finding the workers to complete each task in the church we must learn how to trust God to know how to get the greatest effort out of each. Giving someone a job is not so hard if we pray and search out the Lord for them. Yet it has been my experience that to turn someone loose with the responsibility is another matter. Constantly we hinder the work by wanting our way of doing it perfected. For anyone to step out of the boundaries that we set just can not happen even if they did hear from God as to how to do the job. It is hard to release the reigns and allow someone to gain the victory over a job well done. It is hard to think that anyone can do a better job then we can. Even to admit the possibility is hard for us to do. Yet every body states how humble we are and we are not fretful of someone getting the recognition. Our ability to allow someone to hear from God and complete any task on their own only will show what great confidence we have in God and His choice of the person for the job. That is when you know that you have matured in The Lord and you are ready for the greater works that He has for you.

There are many different ways and avenues to search out to be able to help in any church. The hardest is to find the best place for you and that will only be found in deep prayer as you listen to The Lord. Too often we tell the Lord what we want and pray that He goes along with it. When a pastor does not see the wishes that we have we will declare that he missed God. Agreed sometimes that happens but more often that not God wants you to serve in a different capacity. What I have found the most is people declare that there is no job that they can do in the church. So they do nothing. There has been nothing farther than that from the truth. The greatest job and anointing in the church is soul winners and prayer worriers. Here are two places that we all need to get involved in and continue to work at all the days of our lives. Without these two jobs getting done or working we will not survive as an active church. Our church of old failed in these areas and we found nothing but destruction on our door steps. Our focus turned to each other instead of Jesus and nothing could survive nor would God have let us go on that way. Actually I praise Him for what happened in the church for it changed me for ever. I will not look to man for the result of spirituality. I will seek Jesus and His righteousness and find the answers at His mouth not dependant upon man. I have found that man's idea of truth and God's are seldom the same unless they have heard from God. Plus I have heard His voice clearer than ever and long for every minute that He will give me to live my life with Jesus. That is the answer for the church, live with Jesus and pray for the results of soul winning. Pray for to be used in these two vital fields.

Every person can be a winner in the ways of God if they just simply set their heart on being a soul winner. Over and over again Jesus cried for labors in the field so that the harvest could be brought in to Him. Jesus can save, heal, restore or keep anyone that comes to Him through the cross of Calvary. There is no looser when it comes to making an effort to reach the lost. We do have some that are more talented or anointed but without fail Jesus will anoint anyone that makes an effort. You see we reach people by letter you open your mouth and let her fly. Simply put just tell what Jesus has done for you and how it made a difference in your life with Him in your heart. Tell of the turmoil that became or is becoming peaceful. Tell of the chaos that seems to have taken on order and purpose. Tell of the happiness that comes from being forgiven of your sins and the knowledge of going to heaven when you die. Tell of the lack of fear of death that has been overcome with joy. Tell of the peace of mind that comes from knowing that Jesus is with you no matter what you have to face in this world. Tell of the healings that has happened in your mind and body since you came to Jesus. That is witnessing! That is all you have to do, though remember to invite people to church where they can find out more about Jesus. Amen?

There is always one thing to keep in mind and many people seem to get wrapped up into everything else. Salvation is the greatest miracle that Jesus paid for and nothing else can compare. We can never loose sight of the great commission and seek anything over that. Yet there are some mighty promises in the scriptures that we can have if only we could understand all that Jesus has prepared for us. The blind has a problem of not seeing either spiritually, mentally or physically. This can be eliminated by simple means of knowing what and how Jesus paid for this type of healing. As we look to the cross we see Jesus' death, burial and resurrection to pay for salvation. When we see the payment of the whipping post, Jesus' strips on His back, as clearly as the cross, then His payment of the stripes is for our healing. Because we can see Jesus in this light in the Spirit then we can open our eyes and see our healing of blindness. In the name of Jesus open your eyes and see as Jesus does now! Heart be healed, soul be clean, and body receive your vision as Jesus gives it to you.

One of the greatest revelations that God has given me was about my income and the way to receive it with thanksgiving. Do not shut me out, I have never asked the church for anything except for food and that was before I understood Jesus. In a vision once I saw The Holy Father writing out a check just as if it were a paycheck from any place of employment. He did not show me the amount or a real reason with the exception that His statement was "I am responsible for your income and it will always be enough." Now that left me with the understanding that if God writes the check I am on HIS Time. Where ever He places me to bring in an income I must do the job right and to the best of my ability. I must continue His work until it is done and be the best representative of Jesus that I can be. Perfect, no, but I must strive to do the right thing always. Let me say that again do the right thing always! In so doing God provides the hours, even when I do not think they are enough and the pay. Through my faithfulness to the church, tithes and offerings, not a bill has failed to be paid on time and my name is outstanding in the community. That places my heart in the condition of being thankful of everything I have in this world and with the dearest friend that any man can have, Jesus.

As the years pass by we learn the most important things are not always what you see with your eyes. They are normally what you can see with your heart. The greatest blessing I have other than the Father is my precious wife. All I need is for her to be in the same room and my heart fills completely satisfied. There is a special since of pride knowing that you have made a home that people want to be a part of it. Especially one you love as much as a spouse. Home is something beyond words when it comes to the greatness of God and how He has helped us build. Friends seem to accomplish works that no other team can, Jesus within my precious wife have come a long way from the first day I laid eyes on her. It seems as though we have fulfilled each others life and have surely seen the greatest sharing possible. Neither looks to ourselves first but we look out for the other. There is a special kind of relationship that has something unique like this. When one has this type of relationship to share it does not seem to matter what you have to face. You can endure anything and love even the worst of times as long as you are together. There will never be a time that the hurts in the church would not affect everyone around you. They will cause much doubt, fear and discouragement yet life will go on as you walk with your spouse and Jesus. The victories that you will be able to see will be as you look upon each event and the hurt not be there any more. The love of a good spouse and Jesus will take you to that point if you just simply do not quit.

In the joy of ministering to any one that enters your presence you will also find the pain of the church. Yet I have learned in able to love as Jesus does you must dare to hurt. You may judge only to the point of not being hurt again but never fail to reach out to minister. Those who have hurt you the most is those you have loved the most and when you know that it is over is when they can no longer control your emotions. Then all the world can see how Jesus has come through for you and the person or persons knows they are forgiven. Life is not always fare but you can rest assured that Jesus understands that and he can see us through everything that comes against us. We can hold our heads up high and never be ashamed of the life we have been given. You see we must learn early that it is not about us. Life is about God the Father, the Son Jesus, and The Sweet Holy Ghost. When we enter a relationship through the shed blood of Jesus we have surrendered ourselves and taken up His cause. You see God signs the checks, gives the orders and we follow Him with all the love we can share. That is what life is all about and worth living. All that God gives you other than Himself is blessings including Wife, family, job and church. Let us be about the Father's business and do our part to eliminate all the pain of life we can. Above all let us not be one that causes The Pain in the Church. This should never be acceptable!

Summery

In the previous pages of this book I have attempted to reveal a great need of the unified church. The head of the church is Christ and I feel with all my heart that He wanted this book to reveal how easy it can be to stop the hurt that we impose upon others. Our future depends upon the generation coming up behind us and if they do not learn to put a stop to the pain then it will be very hard to build. Even in the mega churches we have cell groups that act as if they were little churches within the larger church. The same things happen here as they do in the small to medium churches. How are we to unite in the end of time if we can not go to church together or fellowship with one another? It is no longer crossing the denominational lines that causes the greatest problems it is the pain we cause either unintentional or on purpose. Even though it has become a norm it should never be acceptable.

In this day and hour the television is revealing the new churches coming up with the concept that, if we do not offend anyone than our church will grow and we are doing the work of God. What is really sad is they are also leaving out the need for salvation through the blood of Jesus for the payment of sin. When we refuse to reveal the sin and accept anything then the blood of Jesus was shed in vain. We have to understand the price of sin and how Jesus paid for it so we do not live that way. Other wise we have no good news to spread. For without the shedding of blood there is no payment for sin and Jesus did so for all of us. As we are able to see Jesus' sacrifice we are obligated to reveal the whole truth of the scriptures and living in sin brings death by our own choice.

If we believe that God raised Jesus from the dead for the forgiveness of sin and confess Jesus as our sacrifice with our mouth we may be saved. For in believing our sins are forgiven and with confession Jesus comes into our heart to live. In the person of The Holy Spirit in our heart our Father can reveal any sin that can hinder our relationship with Our Lord. Through the love and grace of God we can walk in our salvation daily with the precious hope of making Heaven our next home. Let us not hinder others from this walk and live this life pleasing to God the Father, Jesus the Son, and The Sweet Holy Spirit.

Rev. John D. HOUSEWRIGHT
409 EAST 7th Street
Metropolis, Illinois 62960
Email: ibaprayinman@yahoo.com
(618)-524-4547